Office of Scientific Operations

With the conclusion of the traumatic events in 1933 surrounding the shocking affair involving the city of New York and a beast commonly referred to as "King Kong" the president of the United States, Franklin Roosevelt, established the Office of Scientific Operations (OSO). The purpose of the OSO was to monitor, evaluate the level of risk and assist in any manner the mitigation of danger of any and all scientific operations and anomalies. With the rapid pace of scientific discovery this office was given the highest priority and clearance to investigate any potential threats or consequences to the interests of the United States of America.

Office of Scientific Operations Release #3

K McConnell

Published by K McConnell, 2020.

OFFICE OF SCIENTIFIC OPERATIONS RELEASE #3

First edition. August 12, 2020.

ISBN: 979-8230607694

Written by K McConnell.

From the case files of the
Office of Scientific Operations:

Public Release #3A

File #161

1954

Declassified File

Commonly referred to by the public as "Revenge of the Creature"

1

Jonathon Wyatt wiped the sweat from his brow, pushing his light brown hair aside. It was July in Florida and even with the windows down the breeze wasn't cooling him down.

"You know they make cars with air conditioning." Wyatt said.

"I didn't pick this car." Thomas Wayne, Wyatt's partner at the OSO, said as he drove. "It's a company vehicle."

"Seems like we could afford something a little newer." Wyatt said.

"The budget of the OSO is a tightly controlled apparatus." Wayne said casually. His dark hair was parted down the middle and just long enough to drop a little on to his forehead.

"It's about as hot here as Indonesia was." Wyatt commented.

"Nice vacation, huh?" Wayne asked with a smile.

"Vacation, my ass." Wyatt shook his head. "Is that how most vacations at the OSO go?"

"I don't know. I've never taken a vacation." Wayne said.

"Never? You've been at the OSO for, what, like four years?" Wyatt asked.

"About that." Wayne said. "What would I do on a vacation?"

"I don't know. Relax, I guess." Wyatt said.

"I'm relaxed now." Wayne said.

Wyatt sighed. "OK, well maybe you could meet someone."

"Ah, like you did in Indonesia? That girl..." Wayne said.

"Wanda. Yeah. Only maybe not while trying to avoid being eaten by large prehistoric carnivorous birds." Wyatt said.

"Hmm, yeah, I could live without being killed." Wayne smiled at his own joke.

"Those people last year in the Amazon swore this creature was dead. How is it now someone has captured the thing and is bringing it up here?" Wyatt asked.

"I don't know. They assured us the creature had been shot multiple times." Wayne said.

Wyatt reached back and pulled the file off the back seat for about the tenth time since they had left Washington the day before. He flipped open the cover and started skimming the pages again.

"So we're supposed to meet up with this Joe Hayes guy. He's the one that captured the creature." Wyatt said.

"That's the plan." Wayne replied.

"And we are just...verifying the security set up." Wyatt said.

"I would think this wouldn't take more than a day or two. We just need to make sure they have taken all necessary precautions to ensure this creature doesn't escape." Wayne said.

"The Director said we were to evaluate how dangerous this creature is as well." Wyatt pointed out.

"There's that too." Wayne agreed.

"It's right up here." Wyatt said pointing towards the entrance to Ocean Harbor, a research facility that also doubled as a tourist attraction.

"I see it." Wayne said glancing at his watch. "We're running about fifteen minutes behind schedule."

Wyatt glanced over at Wayne. "You know you're a little obsessed with numbers?"

"I guess." Wayne said.

"No, that's just it, you rarely guess." Wyatt said with a smile.

They pulled in to the parking lot, got out and walked up to the entrance. They showed their credentials and were directed to a large tank across the park. By the time they reached what was called the "receiving" tank there were people all around and a crane was lifting something out of the back of a truck. There was someone on a PA system describing what was happening for the people gathered there. As they drew closer Wayne and Wyatt could see webbed and clawed hands and feet sticking out of the stretcher the crane was lifting.

"That's pretty big." Wyatt said. "What do you think, maybe seven feet?"

Wayne nodded. "Seven and a half, I would say."

They circled around to a set of stairs that led up to the top of the tank where they could view the creature being lowered into the water. People lined the edge of watching the progress of what people were referring to as the "Gillman". After a checking with a staff member they were directed to Jackson Foster, the owner of the facility.

"Oh, you're the government guys I was told about." Foster said shaking their hands.

"Yes sir." Wayne said.

"You're here to make sure everything is safe, as I understand it." Foster said turning back to watch the creature as it was lowered into the tank.

"Yes sir." Wayne replied. "Just verifying the level of risk."

"Well, I think you'll find we've taken every precaution and have everything in hand." Foster said. In a cheery, but dismissive kind of way.

Once the creature was lowered into the water it was pulled free of the stretcher by a man, presumably Joe Hayes. The creature floated face down in the water while Hayes slowly guided it around the tank. There were photographers and film cameras perched around the tank interspersed with the people providing a considerable amount of news coverage.

Wayne and Wyatt watched Hayes walk the inert body of the Gillman around the tank. Nothing much seemed to be happening.

"Are they sure this thing is going to wake up?" Wyatt asked.

Wayne shrugged. "I asked that Gibson guy, the public relations director here, but he said they didn't really know."

"Well, I can safely tell you what the risk level is of a dead creature." Wyatt said.

Wayne nodded. "That's true."

It took about two hours of floating the Gillman around before Hayes called up to watch out because it was starting to wake up. When he did finally fully wake up he stood up and began flailing about. It was obvious the creature was confused and reacting violently.

Hayes scrambled up and out of the tank. He started calling ropes and other equipment in order to restrain the creature. In the tank the creature began thrashing about and then diving underwater. It seemed to be searching for a means of escape from the tank.

Suddenly the creature surfaced and leaped up, grabbing the side of the tank and pulling itself up. It was nearly out of the tank by the time Hayes had grabbed a boat hook and circled around to try to stop it. As Hayes wrestled with the creature Wayne and Wyatt drew their guns out. Each member of the OSO was sent out into the field with .45.

Wayne and Wyatt exchanged looks. They weren't sure what they should do about this situation. Protecting people from creatures such as this was a large part of what they did, but this creature was the property of Ocean Harbor and an object of scientific research. Killing it would have to be a last resort, but they would do it if the lives of people were at stake. The trick was determining when that moment had arrived.

They started to move closer, unsure of when or if they could take a shot at the Gillman if they needed to. Before they could move much closer the Gillman pulled Hayes over the railing and back into the tank. This changed the situation for them. At this point, only Hayes, the man in charge of securing the creature was the only one in immediate danger. They stopped and stood watching the scene unfold as Hayes wrestled with the Gillman in the water. Two other Ocean Harbor workers jumped in and as soon as Hayes was free from the Gillman's grasp they helped Hayes over to the ladder.

They reached the ladder, but the creature attacked them as Hayes climbed out. Both of the Ocean Harbor workers were pulled back into the middle of the tank by the Gillman. Hayes called for some of the other safety guys to throw a net over the creature.

The Gillman thrashed about in anger entangling himself even more into the heavy fishing net. Within minutes they had the creature tied up in ropes and netting. Wayne and Wyatt slid their guns quietly away. It was a relief to not have to make the difficult call about killing the Gillman.

"That creature seems pretty violent." Wayne observed.

"It's just confused." Wyatt said. He could draw on his background as a zoologist to try to get some kind of understanding about what exactly this creature was. It certainly didn't seem to fit into any evolutionary line that Wyatt could remember reading about.

After some quick preparation several divers, including Hayes, went back into the Receiving Tank and slowly moved the Gillman from there, through a short underwater tunnel and into a much larger tank. The second tank already held numerous other fish.

Once in the bigger tank, while still trapped inside the netting, the creature was shackled with a heavy chain to the bottom of the tank. There was sufficient length of chain to allow the creature swim around most of the tank, but not enough to permit it to climb out.

The divers emerged from the water and climbed up out of the tank. At that point it was deemed safe to pull the net off the Gillman. Wayne and Wyatt watched the creature repeatedly swimming to the end of the chain and being jerked backwards. It spent quite awhile attempting to free itself from the manacle around its ankle or trying to pull the chain out of its mooring on the bottom of the tank.

“So, any first impressions?” Wayne asked Wyatt.

Wyatt was leaning on the cement railing that ran around the top of the tank. He stared down into the water. Fascinated by the Gillman.

“I don’t know.” Wyatt said shaking his head. “It just doesn’t fit into any logical place in the current classification of the animal kingdom.”

“It would be nice if we had some sense of its capabilities.” Wayne said watching the Gillman battling the chain that held him.

“Hayes is over there pulling his air tank off. obviously he has had several close encounters with the creature. If anyone knows about this thing, he should.” Wyatt said.

“Agreed.” Wayne said and the two of them made their way around the perimeter of the tank to Hayes.

“Mr. Hayes?” Wayne said as they stood in front of Hayes while he checked the valves on his air tank for damage.

“Yeah.” Hayes answered hardly looking up.

“I am District Investigator Wayne and this is DI Wyatt.” Wayne said.

Hayes looked up at them. “The government guys. Heard you were going to be here. You’re here to make sure we don’t let this guy,” Hayes waved back over his shoulder towards the tank, “get loose, right?”

“Something like that.” Wyatt said. “And a few other things as well.”

“Oh, like what?” Hayes asked, standing up.

“We have to evaluate exactly how dangerous this creature might be.” Wayne said.

Hayes chuckled. “Well, I can tell you first hand he can be pretty damned dangerous. He’s aggressive, very strong, he has sharp claws and his armored skin makes it hard for anything, including bullets, to hurt him very easily. We had to use dynamite down in the Amazon to catch him there, but it nearly killed him, I think, so I don’t think we’ll try that again. Can’t afford to kill off our paycheck.” Hayes smiled at them.

“Right.” Wyatt said, not smiling. He didn’t like the attitude that animals were just something to be exploited for money.

"So what is the plan if this Gillman gets free of the chain and out of the tank?" Wayne asked. His background was in math and physics and he tended be only interested in the end result.

Hayes gave a shrug. "Catch him and toss him back in the tank."

Wayne glanced over at Wyatt. They exchanged a look that they both recognized that Hayes had no real plan to protect any bystanders or the general public from this creature.

"Well, if you will excuse us, we have other matters to attend to." Wayne said coolly.

"Sure." Hayes said with a smile. "See you around, G-Men."

Wayne and Wyatt walked away.

"That guy's cavalier attitude is going to get someone killed." Wyatt said.

Wayne nodded. "I would agree. I think it would be prudent for us to put a call in to the Director and find out exactly what latitude we have in making sure this creature is secure."

"You think we may have to seize the creature?" Wyatt asked.

Wayne shrugged. "I don't know. I hope not. I'm sure Foster would raise hell if we did. He would likely file a lawsuit."

"Well, that won't get him anywhere." Wyatt said.

"No." Wayne said flatly. "The OSO is not subject to the civil codes of the United States. Still, it's best if we could avoid that kind of publicity."

"Right. Well, maybe we can convince Foster that it would in everyone's best interest if he improved his security here." Wyatt said.

"Agreed." Wayne said as they headed down the stairs away from the tank.

2

"So you asked him about the issue of seizing the Gillman?" Wyatt asked.

"I did." Wayne said. "He agrees that the current situation is not acceptable."

"So we need to talk to Foster about it." Wyatt said.

Wayne nodded. "Yeah. It's the first order of business today."

The two of them walked through the Ocean Harbor park towards the Administrative building. Once inside the receptionist said she would check with Mr. Foster about meeting with them. They stood in the lobby of the building and waited while the woman walked back down a hall. Minutes passed and the woman reappeared.

She smiled at them. "I'm sorry, Mr. Foster is very busy today. He sends his regrets, but he asked that you make an appointment and he will be glad to see you then." She stood staring at them, still smiling.

Wayne seemed to be considering his options.

"Ma'am, please go back down to Mr. Foster and ask him if he would like us to shut the park down while we seize the Gillman or leave it open while we haul the creature away." Wyatt said.

The woman's mouth open, but no words came out. She slowly closed her mouth. "I...uh..."

Wayne glanced over at Wyatt, but gave no hint at his surprise at Wyatt's tack.

The woman really wanted to say something, but instead she just turned and walked back down the hall. A moment later Foster came bustling down the hall to the lobby. He looked thoroughly pissed.

"Ah, good to see an appointment time has opened up." Wyatt said.

Wayne suppressed a grin.

"Who the hell do you think you are? Who gave you the authority to come in here and threaten me?" Foster spit out. The receptionist shrank back. It was obvious this wasn't the first time she'd seen Foster like this.

"Uh, let's see, the OSO to the first question and President Eisenhower to the second question." Wyatt said.

Foster fumed for a moment and then turned towards the hall behind him. "Gibson!" He yelled down the hall.

A moment passed and Gibson, the public relations guy, hustled down the hall and joined them.

"Yes, Mr. Foster?" Gibson asked.

"These two...gentlemen seemed to think they have the authority to shut down the whole damned park and take our Gillman." Foster said.

Gibson glanced over at Wayne and Wyatt. He looked back at Foster uncomfortably. He turned slightly indicating to Foster to turn as well. With their backs to Wayne and Wyatt, Gibson talked quietly to Foster.

"What? What the hell are you saying?" Foster could be heard saying. He was having great difficulty talking quietly.

Gibson spoke some more.

"The hell you say!" Foster stamped a foot.

They stood quietly looking at each other for a moment. Gibson nodded to Foster, confirming something. They turned back around.

Speaking through gritted teeth Foster stared straight at Wayne and Wyatt. "So you're taking the Gillman?"

Wayne shook his head. "No. That is not our intent."

Confusion flooded across Foster's features. "But...you told..." He pointed at the receptionist who seemed to cringe when he half turned towards her.

"We just needed your undivided attention to discuss some security concerns we have." Wyatt said.

"So...you're not taking the Gillman away?" Foster asked again.

"Not unless our security concerns are not addressed." Wayne said.

"Oh, well, I certainly have time to talk about any issues you have with our security." Foster, now contrite, said.

"Ah, it sounded like your schedule was kind of full." Wyatt said, trying not to grin.

"Nonsense." Foster glared at the receptionist, who took a step back and stumbled into the desk behind her. "I am always at the disposal of the O...you guys. Do...you know the President personally?" Foster asked politely.

"We golf every weekend." Wyatt said.

"You do?" Foster asked, impressed.

"No. He's just bullshitting you now." Wayne said.

Gibson suppressed a snicker. Foster was clearly irritated at being made to look gullible, but said nothing. He gestured for them to follow him down the hall to his office.

3

"Can't say I'm overwhelmed with the increased security Foster promised to implement." Wyatt said looking around the perimeter of the tank as the two scientists, a short distance away, pulled on their scuba equipment.

Wayne sighed. "I'm not either. He told me this morning he was still working out some of the details of increasing the personnel needed to monitor the Gillman 24 hours a day."

"Well, my gut tells me Foster is dragging his feet. He just doesn't want to pay for the extra people and equipment he needs to get in here." Wyatt said.

"I agree. I think, though, we will have to give him time for all of his excuses to run out. In the mean time, you and I may need to provide the extra security missing here." Wayne said.

"I guess." Wyatt said. "Anyway, I am curious what this Professor Ferguson has in mind for this creature."

"You said that yesterday. I thought you talked to him already." Wayne said.

Wyatt shook his head. "Not yet. He's been busy getting his equipment prepared and...well, hovering around that grad student that's helping him."

"Ah, that Dobson girl?" Wayne asked.

"Yeah." Wyatt answered.

"Well, he better be paying attention to that creature once he gets into that tank and not getting distracted by a girl in a bathing suit." Wayne commented.

They watched as Clete Ferguson, a professor of behavioral science brought in to study the creature, and Helen Dobson, a grad student working on a thesis in marine biology, climbed into the tank. Dobson went in first carrying a small cage that contained some fish. Ferguson followed. He had a long rod with a cable spooling out behind him.

"Is that rod electrical?" Wayne asked.

"Looks like it." Wyatt confirmed.

"What's he going to do with that?" Wayne asked.

"Not sure. Maybe protection. Maybe he's going to use it to control the creature." Wyatt guessed.

"There's no way he can wield that rod fast enough underwater to be useful as protection if that creature gets close enough to him." Wayne pointed out.

"Hey guys." Gibson said walking up to Wayne and Wyatt as they leaned on the cement railing above the tank.

"Afternoon." Wyatt said.

Wayne nodded a greeting to Gibson.

"They started doing anything yet?" Gibson asked.

"Not yet." Wyatt said. "Not exactly sure what they are planning on doing."

"Oh, Clete told me they just wanted to establish some basic ground rules for the Gillman." Gibson said.

Wyatt chuckled a little.

"What?" Gibson asked.

"Well, it's just that humans always think they set the rules, but it often seems like the animals somehow to manage to set their own rules about how things are going to be." Wyatt said.

They watched as Ferguson zapped the creature as it drew near. The creature quickly retreated. It stayed back at the end of it's chain watching Ferguson and Dobson cautiously.

"Guess that was the first rule." Gibson said laughing. "Don't get too close."

"Or the rule as the creature sees it is, if you want to shred the shit out of this guy you will need to catch him when the rod is out of his hands." Wyatt said with a smile.

"Whoa." Gibson looked over at Wyatt. "That's a pretty dark way of looking at it."

Wyatt shook his head. "No. Just different. Your Gillman doesn't think like we do so interpreting how he sees Ferguson and that electrical rod is a guessing game. Unless, of course, you can think like a Gillman."

"Ah, I see what you mean. Yeah, I guarantee you I don't know what's going on in his brain." Gibson said.

They watched as the creature approached the fish cage and Dobson used the microphone system hooked up in her diving mask to order the creature to stop. The creature, of course, kept swimming towards the fish cage and Ferguson used the rod to zap the Gillman again. This time the creature only retreated a short distance, turned around and came back towards Ferguson and the cage. Again Dobson ordered him to stop and again Ferguson gave the creature a shock when he drew close. Turning the creature swam away and then turned again. Dobson called out to stop and Ferguson reached out with the rod, but the creature pulled up short. He hovered just outside the reach of the rod.

"Are they studying it or training it?" Wayne asked.

"I would like to think they are trying to assess how quickly it learns. As a gauge of it's intelligence. But...truth is it's hard to study the behavior of something if you are heavily influencing that behavior." Wyatt said.

"Or if your agenda isn't entirely based on science." Wayne said.

Wyatt looked over at Wayne. "You think there's a plan to have the Gillman doing flips for fish?"

Wayne shrugged. "Don't know. You might ask our friend here." Wayne and Wyatt looked over at Gibson.

"Who me?" Gibson said, looking as innocent as possible. "I'm just the PR guy."

"Right." Wayne said.

"You've got to be kidding me." Wyatt said.

"Our job is security. Not ethics." Wayne said.

"I know, but they find something like this and turn it into a circus show. What the hell." Wyatt said disgustedly.

"Gentlemen. I assure you that Mr. Foster is dedicated to allowing the scientists all the access they desire to this creature." Gibson said.

Ferguson and Dobson were emerging from the tank. A couple of guys helped with their equipment.

"I'm going to talk to Professor Ferguson." Wyatt said and walked away.

"I'm serious about Mr. Foster wanting scientists to study this creature." Gibson insisted.

"And is he planning on training the Gillman for shows?" Wayne asked pointedly.

"Uh, I can't really say what Mr. Foster's ultimate plans are for the Gillman." Gibson said, his gaze turning away to stare down into the water.

"Right." Wayne said. "Well, I guess we'll see if the primary motivation for having the Gillman here is science or money."

"Do they have to be separate things?" Gibson asked.

Wayne nodded. "Yeah. Pretty much. Sooner or later they come into conflict and, generally, science loses out to greed."

"Wow. You guys are really pessimistic." Gibson said.

Wayne shook his head. "No sir. We are paid to see everything as it really is. Not as people want to believe it is or how they want us to see it. Our objectivity is the only way we can do our job effectively. We have to be able to assess situations in the cold light of day in order to determine what's really a danger and what is just a perception of danger."

"OK...well, I guess I can see that. That seems like a hard standard to maintain." Gibson said.

Wayne smiled a little. "Especially when you're being chased by a monster."

Gibson's eyes widened a little. "Does that happen often?"

Wayne gave a slight shrug. "Yeah. It kind of does."

"Whoa. I wouldn't want your job." Gibson said.

"Most people don't." Wayne said. "Excuse me. I would like to go meet these scientists of yours."

"Sure." Gibson said as Wayne walked away.

4

"That's preposterous!" Ferguson said to Wyatt as Wayne walked up to them.

Wyatt shook his head. "No. It's not. It would hardly be the first time that science had to make a compromise to achieve it's goals."

"Mr. Wyatt, I have followed Dr. Ferguson's career for some time now and I can tell you that he is devoted to his work and not to any financial gain." Helen Dobson, the grad student said fervently.

Ferguson looked at her. "Thank you Helen."

"Well, it's true." Helen said, still irritated at Wyatt's insinuation.

"What is true?" Wayne asked. He extended his hand out to Ferguson. "District Investigator Thomas Wayne."

Ferguson shook his hand. "Your partner here was suggesting that our work might be aimed at turning the Gillman into a circus attraction for the tourists."

Wayne glanced briefly at Wyatt. "Well, as a trained zoologist, DI Wyatt is always sensitive to the ethics of science."

"Well, the thought that we would be participating in the *taming* of the Gillman so Ocean Harbor could make money off of him is, well, ridiculous." Ferguson said indignantly.

"Let me ask you something." Wayne said. "How well do you know Foster, the owner of Ocean Harbor?"

Ferguson hesitated. He could see where this question was headed. "I...only just met him for the first time a few days ago."

"So, how certain can you be about his motives?" Wayne asked.

"Why, you're just as bad as him." Helen said pointing at Wyatt.

Ferguson held up a hand towards Helen. "It's alright Helen. They're right. I can't say for certain what Foster's ultimate plans are for the Gillman, but I can tell you this much, everything I do here is to further our understanding of this creature and not to turn this thing into a tourist attraction show."

"That's good to hear." Wyatt said.

Everyone was quiet for a moment.

"So...I thought you guys were some government security guys?" Ferguson said looking at Wyatt.

"We are." Wyatt nodded.

"A zoologist?" Ferguson asked.

"We actually all come from different backgrounds." Wayne said. "The diversity allows us complement our collective knowledge."

"Huh." Ferguson said. "You know that's a really good idea. I don't imagine there are very many government agencies, at least the ones I have dealt with, that have much in the way of diversity in backgrounds."

"Well, most government agencies don't chase monsters." Wyatt said.

Ferguson chuckled. "That's probably true."

“So how comfortable are you when you're in the tank with that thing?” Wayne asked.

“I think once we have established with the creature a healthy respect for the electric rod, I think we should be safe enough.” Ferguson said.

“And if you should lose the rod?” Wyatt asked.

Ferguson smiled. “That's why we are conditioning him to respond to the sound. Soon he'll stop when we stay stop. It's standard behavioral conditioning.”

“I'm not sure this thing falls into the standard model of animals we have ever dealt with before.” Wyatt said.

“Are you sure that you're actually going to be conditioning him to do what you want him to or, if he's smart enough, is he just learning your strengths and weaknesses and biding his time?” Wayne asked.

Ferguson hesitated. “Look, I understand your safety concerns, but what we are trying to do here is establish exactly what his level of intelligence is and there is no way to do that without going down in that tank and interacting with him. I understand the risks involved, but, in my opinion, those are necessary risks.”

Wyatt was going to say something. But Wayne cut him off.

"Alright. Well, we will defer to your experience on these matters." Wayne said diplomatically.

"Thank you." Ferguson said. "Now, if you'll excuse us, we have some notes to write up."

"Sure." Wayne said and, by his body language, indicated to Wyatt to follow him away from the two scientists.

"I think this whole thing is sketchy." Wyatt said when they were far enough away from the two scientists.

"I know what you're thinking. But we are not here to sort out the ethics of what they are doing here." Wayne said.

Wyatt was quiet for a moment. "Yeah. Well, maybe so, but I think Foster is all about the money and I am not certain that Ferguson's motives are entirely focused of the science of this."

"You think he is looking at the prestige this will bring to his career?" Wayne asked.

"I can't rule that out." Wyatt said.

"Well, we aren't here to sort out people's motives for this." Wayne said. "We just need to make sure that the presence of this creature doesn't present a danger to the people here."

"Yeah, but when people's motives are focused on future benefits they tend to lose sight of the issues right in front of them." Wyatt said.

Wayne nodded. "Yeah. I can't argue with that. I just don't think talking about it any further with Ferguson is going to get us anywhere."

"Probably not." Wyatt admitted.

5

“More testing?” Wyatt asked as Ferguson pulled his fins on and checked his mask.

Ferguson nodded. “Yeah.” He sat on the edge of the rail of the tank.

“It sounds like something is on your mind.” Wyatt said.

Ferguson shrugged. “I guess. It’s odd, the tests we’ve run so far indicate that the Gillman is closer to us than to fish.”

Wyatt looked puzzled. “Hmm, well, his body structure is similar to ours, but it’s hard· to see how that would fit into the current evolutionary structure.”

“Exactly.” Ferguson said. “The more we study him the more of an enigma he becomes.”

“You think somehow he doesn’t belong?” Wyatt asked.

Ferguson glanced over at Wyatt. “What do you mean *doesn’t belong*? Like he’s from one of these UFOs that people are so excited about these days?”

Wyatt smiled. “No. Not like some alien creature. I mean that maybe he doesn’t figure into any evolutionary line because he did not evolve naturally to start with.”

“Well, then what are you saying?” Ferguson asked.

“Earlier this year the OSO was involved out west with some ants that had been mutated by atomic testing.” Wyatt suggested.

“Oh yeah, I heard about that. And that dinosaur in New York the year before. Crazy stuff. But, if I remember correctly those ants and the dinosaur were in an area were atomic testing had taken place. There hasn’t been any atomic testing in the Amazon that I know of.” Ferguson said.

Wyatt nodded. “True enough. But that might not be the only way creatures can be altered.”

Ferguson studied Wyatt for a moment. “You...know of some other means of creating creatures like the Gillman?”

"Just speculating." Wyatt said. He really wasn't encouraged by the OSO to discuss the work of Dr. Zeitner back in the 1930s and his manipulation of DNA—and the monsters he had created. It seemed like a stretch to think this creature could somehow be something from Zeitner over 20 years ago, but since much of Zeitner's work had disappeared it was speculated that others may have attempted to reproduce what he was doing. Following along that line, Wyatt thought, what better place to quietly experiment on such things than deep in the jungles of the Amazon?

"I think you know more than you're letting on about these strange creatures we've been seeing lately." Ferguson said. "I think I'd like to hear more about them."

"Another time." Wyatt said as Helen walked up to them.

Helen glanced at Wyatt with a cool nod. She still wasn't happy about Wyatt's questioning of Ferguson's motives.

"Well, I'll leave you two to get to work." Wyatt said and walked part of the way around the tank to where Wayne was waiting to watch today's experiments with the creature.

Ferguson and Helen donned their equipment and climbed into the tank. They began going through their standard routine of behavior testing with the Gillman.

"The creature seems leery of Ferguson and his electric rod now." Wyatt said.

"Maybe." Wayne replied. "Or maybe he's smarter than they think."

"You think he's got a plan?" Wyatt asked.

"Hard to say." Wayne answered.

They watched for a few minutes longer as the test seemed to be going well. Helen was able to issue a command of "Stop!" through the underwater sound system and the creature stopped moving towards the ball Helen waved at the end of a short pole. They tried the experiment a second time.

"I don't like this." Wayne said quietly.

"I agree. He's acting like he's trying to lure her further from the electric rod." Wyatt said.

"Yeah." Wayne said watching intently.

"If this goes badly I'm not sure what we could do from here." Wyatt pointed out.

"Not much." Wayne agreed.

They watched as the creature suddenly darted forward and, ignoring the ball, grabbed Helen. The creature began swimming further away in the tank dragging Helen with it. Helen continued to issue the "Stop!" command, but the creature was ignoring her. Ferguson swam forward as fast as he could with the rod outstretched. He closed on the creature and gave it a shock. The Gillman let Helen go and turned on Ferguson, knocking the electric rod aside. The two of them began wrestling on the bottom of the tank with the creature pulling the mask and regulator from Ferguson's face.

Wayne and Wyatt could do nothing but watch the scene. They could hear through the sound system Helen continuing to order the creature to "Stop!". Finally, the creature let Ferguson go and turned to look at Helen. Thinking quickly she swam as fast as she could towards the far end of the tank joining Ferguson on the surface as they approached the spot they climbed in and out of the water.

The chain prevented the Gillman from catching up to the two of them. Turning back the creature fought furiously against the chain.

Hayes and Gibson helped Ferguson and Helen get out of the water and over the cement rail. Suddenly Gibson called out and pointed. It was obvious the creature had somehow broken the chain. Wayne and Wyatt watched as the creature lunged up at Hayes and Gibson who stood on the ledge on the inside of the rail. Hayes grabbed a pole from one of the attendants at the side of the rail and began pushing the creature back down. He was able to get the Gillman back underwater, but threw himself off balance and fell into the tank. Immediately the creature attacked him.

Wayne and Wyatt each drew their .45s, but there was little they could do. Hayes and the creature were now at the bottom of the tank. They wrestled for a moment longer and then Hayes was still. The creature turned, made for the surface and then leaped out of the water and on the ledge. It was then things got really ugly.

Panic struck the people gathered around the tank and people began fleeing in all directions. The creature climbed over the rail and began moving along the walkway. Wayne and Wyatt tried to move towards the creature, but the panicked crowd blocked them. By the time they could wrangle their way through the crowd the creature had left the area of the tank and was moving towards one of the gates.

Wayne and Wyatt scrambled after the Gillman. From a distance they saw it exit the gate on the ocean side of the park. By the time they reached the gate and crossed the road they watched the creature already wading waist deep into the ocean. There was no way they were going to catch up with him now.

Wayne scanned the beach. Further along he spotted a small motor boat someone had pulled up on to shore. He pointed and with a nod Wyatt followed him to it. They pulled up the beach anchor and pushed the boat back into the water. When it was deep enough they jumped in and Wayne got the engine going.

Wayne turned the boat and headed into the general area where they had last seen the Gillman walking into the water.

"Any ideas?" Wayne said turning the boat in a circle.

"Not really. If I were guessing I would—-there!" Wyatt pointed further out and south of where they were.

Wayne spotted a dark shape breaking the surface and then diving back down. He pointed the boat towards it. In another minute they were at the place, but they didn't see him.

Suddenly Wyatt fired two shots into the water just forward and to their right.

"Did you get him?" Wayne asked. He couldn't see well immediately in front of the boat because the boat was a little tipped up in the front.

Wyatt shook his head. "I don't know. I don't think so. No blood."

"Hayes said bullets didn't have much effect on him." Wayne said.

Wyatt swung around to the left. "There!" He fired twice more as the creature's head again appeared briefly above the water.

"No. I'm sure I missed him that time. The water is too choppy to get off a clean shot." Wyatt said.

"Why did he surface? He could have just swam away. He doesn't need to come up for air." Wayne said.

Suddenly the left side of the boat lurched up. Wyatt fell backwards and out of the right side of the boat. Wayne held on for another moment until the boat was starting to tip completely over and then he went into the ocean as well.

Wyatt surfaced and looked around. He was mentally preparing himself to fight the Gillman in the water—-which would be a very one sided fight. He saw Wayne surface only a few feet away.

"Where is he?" Wayne gasped out. His head swiveled around. He too was expecting a fight.

"Don't know." Wyatt said. He scanned the water all around, but saw nothing except the over turned boat.

Minutes passed while Wayne and Wyatt treaded water.

"I think he's gone." Wyatt said.

"Apparently so." Wayne agreed. "Well, now I know why he surfaced."

"To get a look at us." Wyatt said.

"Right." Wayne said.

"Damn." Wyatt said.

"What?" Wayne asked.

"Something just hit my leg." Wyatt said.

"Is it him?" Wayne asked.

"Hang on." Wyatt ducked under the surface briefly.

Wyatt spit water when he broke the surface again. "It's not him."

"Then what was it?" Wayne asked.

"Shark." Wyatt said.

"Did he bite you?" Wayne asked.

"No. But I think he's thinking it over." Wyatt said. "I think we should get moving towards shore."

"Yeah. Probably—-shit." Wayne said. "I think your friend is checking me out now."

Wyatt stuck his head underwater again and then pulled back up. "Nope. You have your own following."

"Great." Wayne said. "Shall we?" He waved towards the shore.

"After you." Wyatt said.

It took them about ten minutes to swim back to the beach. They crawled up on to the sand and lay there breathing heavy.

Wayne looked over at Wyatt and smiled. "Did you lose your gun?"

"Hell no!" Wyatt said. "The gun I lost in Indonesia cost me two days' pay." He pulled the dripping gun out of it's should holster.

"I jammed this puppy hard into the holster the moment I hit the water." Wyatt held the gun up.

Wayne nodded. "Monsters be damned. The only true evil in this world is the almighty expense report."

"No shit." Wyatt said in agreement.

6

"Well, it's bigger." Wyatt said looking at the boat.

"Yeah. Untie us and let's get going." Wayne said.

Wyatt untied the bow and the stern and hopped into the boat. It had a small cabin forward and a winch secured to the stern. It was, from the equipment laying around inside of it, someone's small fishing vessel.

"Did the Director indicate how far or how long we are supposed to search for the creature?" Wyatt asked.

Wayne shook his head as he drove the boat away from the pier. "No. Not really. I think he's hoping we'll get lucky and spot him somewhere out here."

"I don't know. It's a big ocean and all we have are a couple of possible sightings that indicate he might be headed south. Not much to go on." Wyatt said.

"I agree, but we need to try." Wayne said.

"Yeah." Wyatt said.

They drove out away from the shoreline and then turned south. Wayne kept the boat at a slow steady pace and both of them scanned in all directions with binoculars. Two hours dragged by.

"Anything?" Wayne asked.

Wyatt lowered his binoculars and looked at Wayne. "Are you thinking I would have seen something and not mention it?"

Wayne shrugged. "Maybe you forgot to say something."

"Right." Wyatt said looking back out towards the ocean without the binoculars. He squinted as the sun reflected off the water. He leaned forward a little and shaded his eyes.

"Turn the boat right a little." Wyatt said.

"It's called starboard. You see something?" Wayne asked as he spun the wheel.

"Not sure, Admiral." Wyatt lifted the binoculars for another look. "There's something over there." Wyatt pointed.

Wayne scanned with his own binoculars. "Well I'll be damned. I think it's him." Wayne pointed the boat in the direction of the shore and pushed the throttle. As the boat drew closer it was obviously the Gillman. He had been scanning the shore until he heard the boat approaching. He spun around and saw them coming closer. In a moment he was back underwater.

"Damn." Wyatt said leaning out over the front of the boat. "He's gone. Once he goes down deep enough there's no way to follow him."

They circled the area for a short while, but didn't spot him again. Once again they moved slowly south. Twice more they caught a glimpse of what they thought was the creature, but he ducked under the waves before they could get close to him.

"The sun's dropping down. It's going to get hard to see him now." Wyatt said.

"Yeah." Wayne agreed.

The sun slid lower and the water grew orange in color. From somewhere on shore and a little further ahead they heard a couple of loud bangs.

Wayne looked at Wyatt. "A gun?"

Wyatt nodded. "I think so." He pointed towards the shore. "Over there."

Wayne turned the boat towards the beach. When the boat ground into the sand a few feet off shore Wyatt tossed the anchor out and they both waded the rest of the way on to the beach. The hesitated and then Wyatt pointed down the beach. They saw the Gillman moving from the manicured sod lawn of someone's yard and out on the beach. They took off at a run towards the creature. From the edge of the yard a man appeared with a gun and fired two more shots at the creature.

By the time Wayne and Wyatt drew near the scene the creature was already waist deep in the ocean. They both drew their guns and fired off shots, but there was no visible reaction from the Gillman. It was difficult to say if their shots were clear misses or simply had no effect on the creature. The Gillman dove and was gone again.

Wayne and Wyatt turned and walked up to the man still standing at the edge of his yard.

"Was that...was that the Gillman monster?" The pudgy ruddy faced middle aged man asked. He stood in his bathrobe and an old revolver still shaking in his hand.

"Yeah. That was him." Wayne acknowledged.

"He just appeared at my window." The man said.

"Well, now you have a story to tell." Wyatt said.

"He might have killed me." The man said, flustered.

"Yeah. That *would* make it harder to tell your story to your friends." Wyatt said.

The man's face looked confused. "Uh...yeah...I guess..."

Wayne looked at Wyatt. "Why do you think he came up on shore? I can't imagine he is missing the company of humans."

"Not sure." Wyatt answered.

"Well, you're the zoologist." Wayne said.

"Yeah, zoologist—-not monster psychologist." Wyatt said. Wyatt stood staring off into the distance for a moment. "Hey, didn't Ferguson say that he thought the creature was showing a certain interest in the girl?"

Wayne nodded. "Yeah. He said something about that. You think the creature is looking for the girl?"

"Maybe." Wyatt said. "I mean, if he just wanted to get away from people and find his way home there would be no reason to come up on shore. He can't breathe up here."

"But why here? We are miles south of Ocean Harbor." Wayne said.

"I doubt he has a clue where he's at. He certainly would have any clue about houses, buildings or roads so there aren't any understandable landmarks for him to orient himself." Wyatt said.

Wayne nodded. "So, he's looking for the girl and totally lost."

“That would be my guess.” Wyatt said.

“I’ll buy that.” Wayne said.

“So now what?” Wyatt asked as the sun dropped below the houses behind them.

Wayne sighed. “I guess it’s back to the boat and slowly southward. The only thing we can hope for tonight is that he makes another venture on to the shore.”

“What about me?” The man asked, still standing in the grass.

Wyatt glanced back at him. “You need to go back in your house and work on your story.”

The man stomped off in a huff.

With some effort Wayne and Wyatt were able to push the boat back out into deeper water started back south at a crawl and mostly watching the shoreline for some kind of disturbance. Darkness descended on them. Wayne found a hand held spotlight in a compartment and Wyatt scanned the water all around them.

Wyatt shook his head. "Our odds of spotting him out here in the dark are next to zero."

"I have been trying to calculate that." Wayne said.

"Oh, good. Finally a use for your degree in mathematics." Wyatt said. "I'm sure whatever figure you come up with will instill me with confidence in our mission here."

"You know a lot of what you say comes across as sarcasm." Wayne observed.

"Really? Imagine that." Wyatt said with a smile. "Hey, what's going on over there."

Wayne couldn't tell where Wyatt was pointing, but he assumed it was the cluster of lights on the shore that had caught his own attention.

"What are all those lights?" Wayne asked.

"I don't...oh, wait, that's A1A. That's the road. Those must be headlights." Wyatt said.

"Well why are they all bunched up like that?" Wayne asked.

"Not sure, but we should probably take a look. Just in case." Wyatt said.

"Agreed." Wayne turned the boat towards shore. They ground into the sand just a short ways from the road and the spot where cars seemed to be stopped in both directions. At that point they could now clearly see in the headlights the creature standing in the middle of the road. It seemed confused.

"It's him." Wyatt said.

"Grab that net laying in the front. Maybe we can get it over him." Wayne said.

Wyatt scooped up the fishing net as he hopped out of the boat.

"I don't think this net will hold him for very long. It's meant for fish, not monsters." Wyatt said as the two of them ran towards the road.

"I know, but it might tie him up long enough for us to think of a plan B." Wayne said.

"Like shooting him?" Wyatt asked.

"Maybe." Wayne said. "Actually, probably."

The people seemed reluctant to leave their cars. They just sat there yelling out the window at the creature and honking their horns. The lights and noise were confusing and disorientating the Gillman. He kept turning first in one direction and then back the other way. He was trying to determine from which direction the danger he saw himself in was going to come from.

Wayne and Wyatt stood at the edge of the road. The Gillman hadn't noticed them.

"Give me the other end of that net. When he looks away the next time we need to rush up and toss this over him." Wayne said.

"OK. Ready." Wyatt said.

About thirty seconds passed and their opportunity presented itself. They raced out into the road and threw the net over the creature. Instantly the creature spun around. The net was loose enough for him to swing his arms out and knock both Wayne and Wyatt backwards on to the pavement.

Just as Wyatt feared the creature easily ripped through the net. Wyatt leaped up to try to pull some of the net that was still intact over the creature. The Gillman swiped at Wyatt knocking back down again, but this time its claws slashed a nasty gash across Wyatt's upper left arm.

The creature did stumble on a section of netting around his feet and staggered into the front of a car. The driver laid on the horn loudly. The creature roared and slammed both hands down onto the hood of the car. The hood buckled and a loud hiss that signaled the engine was damaged.

Wayne drew his gun and fired twice at the creature. It was obvious the bullets hurt when they hit the creature, but no blood was visible and it was quickly apparent that even at close range a .45 couldn't penetrate the armor plated skin of the Gillman.

With another roar the Gillman ran towards the beach. Wayne fired twice more, but, with the increasing distance between him and the creature, those shots had even less effect. For a moment Wayne hesitated. He wanted to pursue the creature, though he had no idea what he could do to stop it, but he realized he needed to see if Wyatt was seriously injured or not.

Wayne knelt down next to where Wyatt was sitting in the road.

"Are you OK?" Wayne asked.

Wyatt held a hand over the wound. "Yeah. Just a cut. Did you get him?"

Wayne shook his head. "No. I know I hit him point blank and I didn't see any discernible damage."

"Damn. That son of a bitch is built like a tank." Wyatt said.

"Yeah. We're going to need something more than these," Wayne held up his .45. "to stop him."

Wyatt twisted around to look at the car behind him. The owner was out of his car now staring at the crushed hood and cursing.

"That's not our expense is it?" Wyatt asked waving towards the car.

Wayne shook his head. "No way. The creature attacked the car as a result of the owner honking the horn. Not our fault."

"Thank God." Wyatt said.

"Let's get that arm stitched up." Wayne said helping Wyatt to his feet.

"What about our friend?" Wyatt asked nodding towards the ocean.

"Forget him. There's no way we can track him in the dark. Besides, what would we do if we did catch up with him. At this point we don't have anything to stop him with. Best we can do is let the Coast Guard know where he was last seen." Wayne said.

"Yeah. You're right. Anyway, we need to talk to the Director. We need a better plan than this." Wyatt said.

"Agreed." Wayne said as they walked off into the sand along side the road.

"Hey!" A voice called out.

Wayne and Wyatt turned around. It was the man with the damaged car.

"Is that thing yours?" The man asked.

"What thing?" Wyatt asked.

"That monster." The man replied.

"No. We just chase them. We don't make them." Wayne told the man.

"Well what about my car?" The man asked waving towards the smashed hood.

"What about it?" Wyatt asked.

"Who do I talk to about it?" The man asked.

Wyatt and Wayne looked at one another.

"Uh...a mechanic?" Wyatt said.

Wayne nodded. "Yeah, I think a mechanic would be the best choice."

"What? What the hell kind of an answer is that? Is something wrong with you guys or what?" The man's voice now was steadily rising.

"Well, truth is, given what we do, yeah, there must be something wrong with us." Wyatt said.

"Can't argue with that." Wayne said and the two of them walked down the beach towards the boat.

7

The morning sun was already hot and the reflection off the water was blinding. The boat chugged slowly south not far from shore. There had no additional reported sightings of the Gillman after the incident on A1A nor anything the following day. This day wasn't looking any more promising.

"You think this thing will stop it?" Wyatt said holding up the M1 Garand rifle.

"I hope so." Wayne said. "The Director said get a military grade rifle, so we'll see."

"Can't say I have much confidence in finding him again." Wyatt said scanning all around the boat with the binoculars. He lowered the glasses and glanced over at the stitches in his left arm. They stung some.

"I'm afraid I'd have to agree. He could be anywhere by now." Wayne said.

"Yeah. the news is saying people are spotting him as far north as Virginia and as far away as Mexico." Wyatt said shaking his head. "They're going to have the Coast Guard chasing every choppy wave in the ocean."

"I'm not sure if people actually think they are seeing the creature or they just want to get their name in the papers." Wayne said.

"Yeah." Wyatt went back to scanning the ocean and shore.

The day drifted by without a sign of the Gillman. By evening they pulled the boat up to a public pier and Wayne put in a call to Marcus. Wyatt stood by listening to Wayne's side of the conversation.

"Yes sir, not a sign of anything."

"No. No reports of anything unusual. We checked with the local police here to see if they had heard of anything, but nobody's seen or heard of the creature."

"Right. It's only an assumption that he was heading back to South America."

"Yeah. He could easily have gone back north. No way to tell until he resurfaces somewhere again. Assuming he does. It's possible we might never see him again."

"Yeah. I know. We never get that lucky."

"We were thinking that maybe we would head back up to Ocean Harbor and talk to that Hayes guy, the one that captured him, and see if he could give us any insight into what this creature might do."

"Oh. Damn. We know he was fighting with the creature just before the monster escaped."

"OK. Right. Ferguson might have some ideas as well. We'll do that."

Wayne hung up the phone.

"What about Hayes?" Wyatt asked.

"Dead. He didn't survive that fight with the creature." Wayne said.

"Damn." Wyatt said.

"The Director says to go talk to Ferguson. I think he is still at Ocean Harbor. We need to get up there before he leaves." Wayne said.

They returned the boat they had rented and drove back up to Ocean Harbor. Ferguson and Helen had just returned from a service for Hayes. They were in the lab talking when Wayne and Wyatt found them.

"Any sign of the Gillman?" Ferguson asked.

"We encountered him a couple of times south of here, but lost him both times. He's...difficult to stop." Wayne said.

Ferguson nodded. "Yeah. He's quite a unique specimen."

"We were hoping you could give us some insight into what he might be thinking or where he might go." Wyatt said.

Ferguson sighed. "I wish I could, but our time with him was cut short. In addition, we only saw him under the confined conditions of the tank. How he might act outside of the tank, well, that could be a whole other matter. Especially if he is regularly encountering humans and our modern world."

Wyatt nodded. "Yeah. That makes sense."

"I wish I could be of more help, but I really don't know what to expect from him at this point." Ferguson said shaking his head.

"We did notice something odd, though." Wayne said.

"Oh. What was that?" Ferguson asked.

"Well, twice he came up on shore. It seemed like he was looking for something, but we couldn't really figure out what he would need from shore or why he would risk coming out of the water." Wayne said.

"Huh. You're right that does seem odd." Ferguson glanced briefly at Helen. She shrugged.

Wyatt looked at Ferguson and then at Helen. "Are you sure he wasn't just looking for someone?

"What are you implying?" Helen asked indignantly.

"Maybe." Ferguson admitted.

"Maybe? Maybe what?" Helen looked at Ferguson.

"Well, I did notice his behavior towards you was...different." Ferguson told her.

"Well, yes, but he was afraid of you because you used the electric rod on him. He didn't have the same fear of me." Helen said.

"Maybe." Ferguson repeated.

"Maybe? Of course that's what it was." Helen said, clearly feeling a little uncomfortable at the suggestion that the Gillman was somehow infatuated with her.

"Well, it was a thought anyway." Wayne said.

"Not a good thought." Helen said.

"Well, anyway, sadly, we might never know what happens to him. Such a loss to science." Ferguson said.

"While I am a firm believer in advancing our scientific knowledge, our mission is to try to eliminate the danger he poses to the public." Wyatt said.

"Of course. Of course. It's important he doesn't harm anyone else." Ferguson said.

“Well, we’ll be off then.” Wayne said and they bid farewell to Ferguson and Helen.

Wayne and Wyatt walked back out and stood in the middle of the park.

"I guess I will call the Director and see what he wants us to do. Why don't you check in with the Coast Guard and see if there's any news." Wayne said.

Wyatt nodded. "Alright."

It took them both about twenty minutes to track down available phones in the Administration building and make their calls. Wyatt hovered in the shade of a tree just outside the Administration building when Wayne came out the door.

"Anything from the Coast Guard?" Wayne asked.

Wyatt shook his head. "Nothing. No sign of him."

"Well, the Director says we are to hang around here for a couple more days. If nothing more turns up we are to head back to Washington." Wayne said.

The following afternoon Wayne waited in a local diner for Wyatt to return from calling the Coast Guard.

"Are you waiting for someone?" The waitress asked holding a menu.

"Yeah." Wayne said. "You can leave the menus. He should be here shortly."

The waitress set the menus down. "So, you're not here waiting for a wife or a girlfriend?"

Wayne looked up at the woman puzzled. "I just said...no I'm not waiting for anyone like that."

"Here on business?" The waitress smiled at Wayne. She had a pleasant smile.

"Uh, yeah, kind of." Wayne said, hesitantly.

"What do you do?" The woman asked.

"I...work for the government." Wayne said.

"The gov'ment." A balding man in the next booth turned around. "Well, if you ask me, you gov'ment guys need to be out catching that Gillman."

"Uh...the government is searching for the Gillman." Wayne said.

"Is that what you are doing here?" The waitress asked.

Wayne sighed. "Yeah. We are under strict orders to search every diner for the creature. We'll know him because he'll order a fish sandwich."

The waitress gave Wayne a nasty look. "Are you trying to be funny?"

"I was trying." Wayne said.

The bald man turned back around. "Gov'ment guys never do anything."

The waitress stomped a foot and huffed.

Wyatt walked in. He came straight to the table, but didn't sit down.

"Coast Guard says there was a possible sighting north of here. Somewhere around Jacksonville." Wyatt said.

"You are hunting that monster." The waitress said.

Wyatt just looked over at the woman.

"Yes, but he is clearly not in here so we will need to move on to the next diner." Wayne said as he stood up.

The waitress stomped away angrily.

"Finally, the gov'ment doing something." The bald man said over his shoulder.

Wyatt looked at Wayne. "What the hell?"

Wayne shook his head. "Never mind. Let's head on up to Jacksonville."

8

"I think it's right up here. Yeah. A right on that street." Wyatt said staring at a map of Jacksonville.

Wayne turned the car down the street. After a couple of more turns they pulled into a driveway and got out. A man came out on the front porch and stared at them.

"Are you Mr. Jameson?" Wayne said walking up to the porch.

"Yup. Who are you?" Jameson asked.

"We're helping the Coast Guard track down this Gillman." Wyatt said.

"OK. Already told the police about it, but I'll tell you too. Come on." The man said with a wave as he walked past them and around the side of the house. Wayne and Wyatt followed him.

Along the side of the house, at the end of the driveway, was a fence gate. The man opened it and the three of them walked into a backyard that ended at a canal. The canal was connected to the St. John's river. The man crossed the backyard to a dock that stuck into the canal.

"Right here." Jameson waved vaguely at the end of the dock.

"You saw the Gillman here? On your dock?" Wyatt asked.

Jameson nodded. "Yup. Right there."

"When was this?" Wayne asked.

"Last evenin'. Bout sunset. Course he was here this mornin' too." Jameson said casually.

"You saw him just this morning? Right here?" Wyatt asked, glancing at Wayne.

Jameson nodded again. "Yup."

"What was he doing?" Wayne asked.

Jameson shrugged. "I don't know. Just standin' there. Lookin' round."

Wyatt eyed Jameson. "And you're sure it was the Gillman?" Wyatt was starting to suspect this man was just looking for some notoriety.

It seemed like an amazing bit of luck that the Gillman would still be hanging around here just waiting for them to show up.

Jameson looked at Wyatt like he was an idiot. "You think I can't tell the difference 'tween a man and a big green walkin' fish?"

Wayne looked at Wyatt. "Why would he be hanging here?"

"Another monster psychology question? Well, I don't know. There must be something around here that is attracting him." Wyatt said.

"Maybe it was those people out on the river." Jameson volunteered.

"What people?" Wayne asked.

Jameson sighed and waved out towards the St. John's river at the end of the canal. "Out there. There was a boat earlier. It broke down and a couple of people jumped off and went swimmin' while it was being fixed. I watched them for a little while. Pretty blonde woman."

"Wasn't...Ferguson and Helen Dobson taking a boat up here today?" Wyatt asked.

"Yeah. You think the creature is stalking her? Wayne asked.

"We suspected that before, but this sure seems like he has become fixated with Helen." Wyatt said.

"Does sound—-" Wayne started to say when a woman's scream came from several houses further along the canal. Both Wayne and Wyatt immediately started running towards the scream. They cut through people's backyards, having to hurtle one small fence. When they reached the yard where the scream came from they saw a woman inside her screened in back porch staring out at the Gillman who was standing just outside the screen.

Wayne and Wyatt stopped. Wayne started pulling out his .45.

"I don't think that's going to do it." Wyatt said.

"We didn't bring the rifle." Wayne said.

"Well, we can't just wander around the neighborhood with an M1. It makes people nervous." Wyatt said.

"Let's see if we can get him away from the woman anyway." Wayne said.

"Agreed." Wyatt replied.

"Hey!" Wayne yelled at the Gillman and started waving his arms.

"Hey, Gillie!" Wyatt yelled, also waving his arms over his head.

"Gillie?" Wayne asked.

"Yeah. I feel like we are kind of on a first name basis now." Wyatt said.

The both of them edged closer and to one side of the Gillman. The creature turned at the sound of their yelling and stared at them. It was clearly confused and unsure if they were a threat or just an annoyance. Finally, with a snarl and a swipe of it's claw the creature turned to fully face Wayne and Wyatt.

"OK. Now what?" Wyatt asked.

"Good question." Wayne replied.

The Gillman glanced over at the woman and then began moving towards Wayne and Wyatt. Fortunately, moving on land was somewhat cumbersome for the creature and running appeared to be out of the question for it. This allowed Wayne and Wyatt to nimbly keep just out of the range of it's claws. A couple of times the frustrated creature made a lunge at one of them, but they were able to duck and twist away from it.

After a few more minutes of this it was apparent the Gillman was getting winded. It's inability to breathe out of the water was taking a toll upon it. Finally, it turned and headed back towards the canal.

"So how are we going to stop it?" Wayne wondered.

"Well, I'm not going to rush up and tackle it." Wyatt said.

"Probably not a good idea." Wayne agreed.

They watched helplessly as the Gillman shuffled to the edge of the canal and dove in. He sank beneath the surface and they didn't see any further sign of him.

"So?" Wyatt asked.

"Well, I guess we know for sure he's here." Wayne said.

"Yeah." Wyatt said.

"You notice something about that woman?" Wayne asked pointing back at the house.

"What's that?" Wyatt asked.

"She was blonde." Wayne said.

"Ah, like Helen Dobson." Wyatt said nodding.

"Right. He's hunting for her." Wayne said.

"And, she's here in Jacksonville. Somewhere." Wyatt said.

"I think we need to find her and at least warn her and Ferguson that the Gillman is here and looking for her. I think I need to call back down to Ocean Harbor and see if anyone there knows where Ferguson and Helen were going to be in Jacksonville." Wayne said.

Wyatt stared out at the calm waters of the canal. "Well, at least it's a plan."

9

Night had fallen as Wayne and Wyatt drove along the river. The radio was on in the event there were any reported sightings of the Gillman.

"It's a shame no one at Ocean Harbor knew where Ferguson and that Dobson girl were going." Wyatt said staring out the window of the car.

"Yeah. That boat captain wasn't any help either." Wayne said.

"So what happens if...nothing happens?" Wyatt asked.

"Not sure. Ferguson flies out later tonight. I guess we would just have to follow Helen Dobson around for a while to see if the creature makes an appearance." Wayne said.

"Well, I guess there are worse assignments than having to follow a beautiful woman around." Wyatt said.

"I thought you had a girlfriend back in Washington." Wayne said.

"I know. I'm just saying, given our typical day at the office following the Dobson girl around would certainly be a change of pace." Wyatt said.

Wayne nodded. "Guess I can't argue with that."

"I mean it's not like—-" Wyatt started to say.

"Wait. What's that?" Wayne reached down and turned up the volume on the radio. The announcer was just saying something about a woman being attacked by the Gillman at a place called the Lobster House on Pier 9.

"That sounds like our friend." Wyatt said.

"I suspect we may find Ferguson and Helen there was well." Wayne said.

They were forced to pull into a gas station and get directions to the Lobster House. It turned out they were quite close to Pier 9 and they arrived only a few minutes later. There was a crowd of people congregated out on the dock at the back of the restaurant. Wayne and

Wyatt made their way through the crowd. Out in the water they could see Ferguson being picked up by a Police boat.

"What happened?" Wayne asked a man standing next to him.

"I...I don't know. All of a sudden the Gillman was walkin' into the place." The man said.

"He grabbed the girl." A woman added.

"What girl?" Wyatt asked, though he already was sure what the answer to that question was.

"Some blonde girl." Another man said.

"Hey, there's something down there!" Someone yelled.

Wayne and Wyatt looked down along the river in the direction the person pointed. Sure enough there was movement along the surface.

"He can't stay underwater with Helen." Wyatt said.

"Right." Wayne said looking around. "There's a boat down towards that end of the pier. Come on."

The two of them wrestled their way through the crowd and ran down to where the boat was, but the boat wasn't tied to the dock. It drifted a short distance off in the water.

"Hmm." Wayne said staring out at the boat.

"I think I can make it." Wyatt said.

"Make what?" Wayne asked.

"Jump out to the boat." Wyatt replied.

"Uh...I don't know about that." Wayne said skeptically.

"Well, while you calculate out the possibility, I'm going to get that boat." Wyatt backed up a few strides.

Wayne shook his head. "I think you're going to be a couple of feet short."

Wyatt glanced over at Wayne and took off running. He leaped off the end of the dock towards the boat. He splashed into the water about four feet short of the boat. He resurfaced and looked back at Wayne.

"That wasn't two feet." Wyatt called out.

"Yeah. Sorry. I didn't account for wind drag." Wayne said as Wyatt swam over to the boat and towed it back to the dock.

They climbed into the boat and started the motor. Slowly they started making their way up the river. It was slow going because the only light on the river came from the surrounding homes and buildings of Jacksonville. They had to watch for fallen trees and debris in the water.

As they crept up river they could hear the sounds of sirens in the distance. Wayne slowed the boat down even more.

"What is it?" Wyatt asked, glancing back at Wayne.

"I think I see something on the shore over there." Wayne pointed. He turned the boat towards shore and slid up on to the sand.

They both hopped out. Wyatt ran over to one of the bodies laying next to a palm tree. Once he got close he didn't need to examine any further to know that the guy was dead. Wayne knelt down next to the other body. He went to check for a pulse along the man's neck, but the limp and wobbly nature of the man's neck immediately told him how this man had died.

"What about that one?" Wayne asked as Wyatt walked over.

"No. It looks like he was snapped in half. I think he was thrown into that tree." Wyatt answered.

"This one's dead too. Neck's broken." Wayne said.

"Should we call this in?" Wyatt asked.

"Not right now. He's got to be close. We need to keep searching for the girl. Assuming she's still alive." Wayne said.

"I'm guessing she is. I don't think he wants to harm her." Wyatt said.

"Agreed. Let's go." Wayne said standing up.

They pushed the boat back out into the water and continued on up the river.

"I think I see someone. Over there." Wyatt pointed towards another sandy spot along the shoreline of the river.

"It looks like a woman." Wayne as he steered in that direction. Before they could close on the spot another figure emerged from the water. It was clearly the Gillman. He reached the staggering woman before Wayne could get the boat to shore. The creature grabbed the woman. She let out a scream and within moments the Gillman was carrying Helen back into the river.

Wayne angled the boat towards the creature, but the engine stalled. Wyatt pulled out his .45.

"That's not going to stop him." Wayne said.

"No, but it might distract him." Wyatt moved around a bit at the front of the boat. "I can't get a clean shot at him."

They watched the Gillman and Helen disappear into the darkness further up river.

"There's pay phone over there. On shore. Let's get this called in." Wayne said.

"I'll go. I'm already wet." Wyatt said tucking his gun away and dropping down into the river. It was shallow enough here that he could walk to shore. A few minutes later Wyatt was back along the shore.

"They said they are organizing up at Point Diego. It's just a little ways further up." Wyatt called out.

"OK. I think I can have this engine going again in a minute." Wayne replied.

"Good." Wyatt waded back out to the boat.

It took Wayne another fifteen minutes to get the engine working. Finally back underway they slowly headed further up the river towards Point Diego. Another ten minutes passed and they closed in on Point Diego. They could see the lights of several vehicles parked there. Before they could pull into the shore a flare lit up the sky from somewhere further along the river.

"Somebody must have found something." Wyatt said.

"Right. Let's go take a look." Wayne said swinging the boat back out into the river.

It took them a few minutes to reach the spot, but they could tell they had found it by the two large mobile searchlights that were illuminating a spot along the shore. As they moved closer Wayne cut the engine. He could see Ferguson on the waters edge using a bullhorn to order the creature to stop. Obviously he was hoping the conditioning they done in the tank would have an effect on the Gillman.

The Gillman was carrying Helen back into the river. He was about waist deep when he seemed to react to Ferguson's commands. He let go of Helen and turned to face Ferguson. Helen crept slowly towards Ferguson then, when they could reach each other, Ferguson pulled Helen up on to the shore. The Gillman grew angry and started approaching, but the crowd of police lining the shore opened fire on the Gillman. Stumbling backwards into the deeper water, the creature disappeared beneath the surface.

The police continued firing into the water for a few minutes more, but no further sign of the creature was seen.

Wayne and Wyatt's boat drifted close to shore and they hopped out to join Ferguson and Helen on the sandy beach.

Ferguson looked at Wayne and Wyatt in surprise. "Where did you guys come from?"

"We've been tracking the creature for days now. Apparently he was following the two of you." Wayne said.

"Yeah. I think we figured that out now." Ferguson said. "I'm just glad Helen is OK."

"You think he's dead?" Wyatt asked.

Ferguson turned to look out at the river. "I don't know. But we aren't staying around to find out." Ferguson glanced down at Helen who only nodded in response.

Wayne and Wyatt stared out at the river as well.

"What are you guys going to do? I mean, this is your kind of thing, isn't it?" Ferguson asked.

Both Wayne and Wyatt nodded while still looking at the clam waters of the St. John's river.

Wayne sighed. "Yeah. This is our kind of thing."

"Well, he's all yours. I hope I never seen him again." Helen spoke up.

Ferguson and Helen, with a brief wave, turned and walked away.

"So, now what?" Wyatt asked.

"Well, I'm thinking in the morning we start dragging the river." Wayne said.

10

Wayne and Wyatt stood on the sandy shore and watched the boats out on the river. The police had been dragging nets along the bottom of the river for more than an hour, but had come up with nothing.

"What did the Director say about Simms and Regan coming down to help hunt for this thing?" Wyatt asked.

Wayne shook his head. "Not coming. He said they were off to Japan."

"Japan." Wyatt said. "What's going on over there that we need to be involved in?"

"Not sure. He said there were sightings of something big in the waters off Japan." Wayne said.

"Another one of those Rhedosaurus?" Wyatt asked.

"Don't know. It sounded pretty big though. The Director offered our assistance in investigating it." Wayne said.

"Well, maybe they'll pull up a body here and we can go home." Wyatt said.

"You don't sound optimistic." Wayne said.

Wyatt shook his head. "No. Not really. This thing seems pretty damned tough to kill. I'm not sure they hurt it enough last night to kill it."

"I'm afraid I have to agree with you on that." Wayne said.

The morning gave way to early afternoon. Finally the local police chief told Wayne and Wyatt that if they hadn't found any body by now it was unlikely they would find anything. It was possible that the body may have drifted down river and into the ocean or an alligator had eaten it. The river dragging was wrapped up and Wayne and Wyatt eventually were the only two left standing along side the river at Point Diego.

"Well, I know that since we didn't find a body, the Director will want us to stick around for a couple more days to see if any sign of the creature shows up." Wayne said.

"Yeah. So I guess we are going to need to stick to the river. If he's dead and washed out to sea or eaten by an alligator we will probably never know what happened to him. If he survived, then he probably will still be looking for Helen Dobson. That means he will show up somewhere along the river looking for her." Wyatt said.

Wayne nodded. "I guess so. So, we'll need another boat."

"Yeah. The only question is which way to go. Up river or down." Wyatt said. "My thought is up river."

"Why up river?" Wayne asked.

"Because the creature was found in fresh water. I think this river is most like his natural habitat. I think it less likely he heads down river into the city and the brackish water at the mouth of the river." Wyatt said.

"Makes sense." Wayne said. "Let's go find ourselves a boat."

It took them about two hours to track down a boat they could rent for a couple of days. The boat came with it's own captain which freed Wayne up to assist Wyatt in searching for the creature. They moved slowly up the river passing Point Diego and further up the St. John.

"Still not quite sure about this guy." Wyatt said quietly to Wayne as they stood at the bow of the boat, each scanning their respective sides of the river.

"Yeah. Well, he was available." Wayne said.

Captain Jack Mack, a short scruffy white haired man, fussed about in the wheel house talking to himself endlessly. He seemed to have only two modes of conduct. He was either moving constantly with boundless energy or sound asleep with his feet propped up.

"That's not exactly a ringing endorsement." Wyatt said.

"Never seen the likes of it!" Captain Jack's voice was suddenly right behind them. Both Wayne and Wyatt jumped at the sound of it.

"The likes of what?" Wayne asked with a sigh.

“The monster! Of course the monster. What else is there? Craziest thing ever. Right here. Right in my backyard.” Captain Jack said. “Damnedest thing ever.”

"Right. You think your net will hold this thing?" Wyatt asked waving a hand towards the heavy fishing net hanging off a spar at the front of the boat.

"That net?" Captain Jack asked. He looked like the question a personal insult. "That net is the finest net in all of Florida. Why, I've caught sharks in that net. Not little sharks either. Great Whites. Giants. 20 foot long. Monsters."

"20 feet long, eh?" Wayne asked. He glanced down the length of Captain Jack's boat. "This boat isn't 20 feet long."

"Ah, you don't need a big boat to catch big fish. Not if you know how to fish." Captain Jack said waving off Wayne's words.

"Well, we are hunting a monster, but it's not a fish." Wyatt said.

"No matter. Captain Jack has caught everything there is in the sea." Captain Jack said.

"You haven't caught this." Wayne said.

Captain Jack reached out and patted the net. "This net can hold a monster. You'll see."

They worked their way up the river through the afternoon, but encountered nothing unusual. The sun was dropping lower in the sky and the shadows began stretching out across the water.

"I am beginning to think that maybe the Gillman is dead." Wyatt said.

"Maybe." Wayne said. "Seems like we would have either seen something or heard something over the radio by now."

"What do you think? Just pull up somewhere along the shore for the night and start again in the morning. These shadows are making it difficult to see much now." Wyatt said.

"Yeah. I guess so." Wayne hesitated. "What is that sound?"

"You hear it too? I thought it was just me." Wyatt said looking around.

"I hear it. Just above the sound of the motor." Wayne said.

"There!" Wyatt pointed towards the shore. There was a woman sitting alongside the water. She seemed to be wailing and crying.

Wayne and Wyatt exchanged a look.

"Captain, steer to the shore!" Wayne yelled back to Captain Jack. He pointed towards the woman. A moment later the boat slowly curved in to the embankment that bordered the river here. When they were close enough both Wayne and Wyatt hopped from the front of the boat on to the grassy shore. They walked over to the woman as she sat weeping.

"Are you OK?" Wyatt asked the woman.

"He's gone." The woman stuttered between sobs.

"Who's gone?" Wayne asked her.

"My husband." The woman said.

"What happened to him?" Wyatt asked.

"He was...he was just sitting here fishing and...and it got him." The woman struggle to get it out.

"What got him?" Wyatt asked.

"I...I think it was an alligator. A big one." The woman said.

Wyatt looked over at Wayne. They were unsure what to do. This wasn't there mission. This was something for the local police to deal with.

"There's some big ones in here. Yes sir." Captain Jack was suddenly right behind Wayne and Wyatt. They turned at the sound of his voice.

"The boat." Wayne said turning to see if there boat was floating down the river.

Captain Jack waved a dismissive hand. "Ah, she's fine. She'll idle right there waiting for us."

"Go anchor that or tie it off somewhere. Can't afford to be chasing that boat all over the county." Wayne said.

"Bah!" Captain Jack said and he waddled back towards the boat as it continued to slowly try to drive itself up on to the shore.

"It was a devil, that gator. Biggest one I've seen in these parts." The woman said.

Wyatt looked at Wayne. "You think it could be him?"

Wayne shrugged. "Ma'am did you get a good look at this alligator?"

"Did it walk on two legs?" Wyatt asked.

The woman looked at Wyatt as if he was crazy. "Two legs? What have you been smoking boy?"

"Did you see the alligator?" Wayne asked the woman.

"Not very well. I saw a dark green thing reach up and pull my poor husband down into the water and drag him under." Woman cried some more.

"How long ago did this happen?" Wyatt asked.

"Half hour ago." The woman said.

Wyatt looked at Wayne. "If it's him, he's probably still around here somewhere."

Wayne nodded. "Maybe we should circle about here a bit and see if we can see anything."

"You know this gator?" The woman asked.

"Maybe." Wayne said.

They walked back down to the boat and hopped back up on to the deck. Captain Jack pulled the boat back from the shore and, at Wayne's direction began a slow circle out into the river. Wayne and Wyatt each took a side and scanned the waters for any sign of human or beast.

"Don't seem right. That is." Captain Jack said.

Wayne sighed. He turned back to look at Captain Jack. "What doesn't seem right?"

"That gator. Pulling a man down into the water like that. They are lazy bastards. They don't go after anythin' they have to fight with." Captain Jack said shaking his head.

"Well, that's why we're staying here. It might not be an alligator." Wayne said.

"It's your monster. I know it is. I feel it in my bones." Captain Jack said nodding.

"If it's good enough for Captain Jack's bones..." Wyatt said over his shoulder as he stared out at the water.

"They never lie." Captain Jack said nodding even more firmly.

"Be the only part of him that doesn't." Wayne mumbled.

"What's that?" Captain Jack asked.

"Just saying I guess I should call in an air strike to bomb this whole river." Wayne said.

"Would they do that?" Captain Jack asked, his eyes wide.

Wyatt laughed. Wayne sighed.

"Would they?" Captain Jack repeated the question.

"No." Wayne answered. "They most certainly will not."

"Ah!" Captain Jack waved a hand disgustedly at Wayne.

They made wider and wider circles that encompassed a larger and larger area both up and down river, but they found nothing. They were using flashlights across the surface of the water in the dim light of the evening by the time they gave up. They dropped anchor not too far off shore from the place where the man had been pulled into the river.

The three of them had settled down in various lounging positions around the small deck and ate Captain Jack's dubious provisions. Afterwards, in the dim light of the single bulb that swayed slowly back and forth in the wheelhouse behind them, they sat and listened to the night sounds of the river.

"Why do you fellas want to find this thing? This monster thing?" Captain Jack asked while lighting up yet another cheap cigar. "If you ask me, this thing, he's gone. Let him go. Good riddance. He sounds like trouble. Captain Jack does not go looking for trouble."

"It's our job." Wyatt said.

"Your job? What kind of a job is it to go looking for monsters? Who makes you take a job like that? Ah, wait—-" Captain Jack held up a hand. "Ex-wives. Yes, yes, Captain Jack understands this. Ex-wives are expensive. I know this. I have many."

Wyatt looked over at Wayne. "Why do I have an easier time believing the possibility that some giant lizard is threatening Tokyo right now than a woman willingly married this man?"

Wayne nodded. "And he said *many*."

Wyatt shook his head. "I have seen some incredible things in this job, but there's a limit to what is realistically possible in this world."

"Yes many. The women. They like Captain Jack." Captain Jack said nodding his head with a smile.

"It cannot be because he talks about himself in the third person because that's just annoying." Wayne said.

"DI Wyatt agrees." Wyatt said with a smile.

"Don't start that shit." Wayne said shaking his head.

"So you hunt the monsters for the money? Yes?" Captain Jack asked.

"No." Wyatt said. "Definitely not for the money."

"Then why? Why do you go look for trouble? If it does not come to you, why go try to find it? This makes no sense to me." Captain Jack said shaking his head.

"We do this because we choose to. Because we feel like it is important. Someone should be watching for things that are a threat to this country." Wayne said.

"So you do this?" Captain Jack asked.

"The Office of Scientific Operations does. It reports to the president of the United States on anything that might be a danger to the country or the people." Wayne answered.

"Office of fools if you ask me. Go out looking for trouble. Nonsense. You wait for trouble to find you. If it doesn't find you, well, then, you have no troubles." Captain Jack said. "And presidents! Don't get me started. They are like wives. They make big promises before you have them and cost you lots of money before they are finally gone."

"An enlightened philosophy." Wyatt said sarcastically.

"I think so." Captain Jack nodded in sincere agreement.

"Well, you might want to think about—-" It was as far as Wayne got before and a deep thud struck the underside of the boat. The three of them rolled from their positions as the boat jerked and then spun slowly around the anchor rope.

"What the hell?" Wyatt scrambled to his feet.

"Something struck the hull." Wayne said as got up and leaned over the side of the boat.

"Probably a log. Sometimes it happens. They fall into the river and float down." Captain Jack said as he leaned out and inspected another section of the boat.

Another resounding thump struck the hull. And the boat started rotating in the opposite direction.

"Another log?" Wyatt asked. "OK, math guy, what are the odds of two logs hitting us?"

Wayne glanced over at Wyatt. "Not likely."

"That didn't sound mathematical." Wyatt said.

"That was not a log." Captain Jack said. He ducked into the wheel house and a moment later reappeared with a revolver in hand.

Wayne looked over at Wyatt and gestured for him to get the rifle.

"What makes you think it wasn't a log?" Wayne asked.

"My bones. They tell me. This is something else." Captain Jack said as he began working his way around the boat watching the water.

"Ah, his bones again." Wayne said as he pulled out his .45.

Wyatt worked another section of the side of the boat. "For whatever reason, his bones won't shut up."

"We're going to need more light. Can't see much out here now." Wayne said.

It was quiet. Wayne and Wyatt had worked their way back up to the bow of the boat. Captain Jack was in the stern.

There was splashing from somewhere towards the back of the boat and Captain Jack's revolver fired three times.

"Damned thing." Captain Jack said.

Wayne and Wyatt looked towards the back.

"What was it?" Wayne asked.

"Don't know. Big thing. Moves fast." Captain Jack answered.

"Did you hit it?" Wyatt asked.

"Don't know. Maybe he's dead. Maybe not." Captain Jack said.

Something hit the boat hard on the port side. The boat rocked. Wayne lost his balanced and started over the rail. Wyatt reached out and grabbed the back of Wayne's shirt. He pulled him back.

"Thanks." Wayne said.

"Whatever that is, I don't think you want to be in the water with it." Wyatt said. He turned to check on Captain Jack who was clinging to the side of the wheelhouse so he didn't fall in.

"I think we can safely say you didn't kill him." Wyatt called back to Captain Jack.

"I am thinking he is still very much alive." Captain Jack acknowledged.

"What do you think Captain, is this our monster or just a very hungry alligator?" Wayne asked.

"No alligator has ever attacked my boat before." Captain Jack said shaking his head. "If this is an alligator he is a big one."

Captain Jack turned away from the water. He stood still for a moment.

"What is it?" Wayne asked Captain Jack.

"Something...is not right." Captain Jack said as he ducked into the wheel house. Wayne and Wyatt could see him lift a hatch and duck down into the hull of the boat. They walked over to the wheelhouse.

"What is it?" Wyatt called down the hatch.

"My boat. She is leaking. The bastard has cracked her beautiful hull." Captain Jack said disgustedly.

"Are we sinking?" Wayne asked.

"I do not think so." Captain Jack said climbing out of the hatch as a humming sound started. "I think the pumps will keep us up."

There was a splashing again on the port side. Wyatt wheeled around and stepped up to the rail. There was a clearly defined swirl of water drawing near the boat. He lifted the rifle and fired twice into the churning water. There was a violent spray of water and whatever it was dove deeper.

Wayne looked over the side of the boat. "Did you hit it?"

"I don't know. Not sure how I could have missed it at this range, but the light is so bad, well, hard to say." Wyatt answered.

On the starboard side now was a splash. Captain Jack fired three times into the water as Wayne joined him along the rail.

"Damn." Wayne said. "We're never going to hit it in this dark. We need more light."

"Wait." Captain Jack said and ducked into the wheelhouse. Suddenly a beam of light shone out across the water from the window of the wheelhouse.

"Great. Bring it here." Wayne called out.

"I cannot." Captain Jack said.

Wayne stepped back into the door of the wheelhouse and saw that the light connected into an outlet next to the wheel. It was tethered to the console.

"It is for me. When I am navigating at night." Captain Jack explained.

There was the sound of splashing water now on the port side.

"Shit!" Wyatt yelled out.

Wayne spun around to see Wyatt twisting around and firing again into the water.

"Damn it. Missed him." Wyatt said.

"He didn't miss you by very much." Wayne said staring at the shredded back of Wyatt's shirt. "And you're bleeding a little.

"Toss a little pain into that and you've got the whole picture." Wyatt said.

"Well we're going to have to—-" The boat was slammed hard again while Wayne was talking.

All three of them were thrown down on to the deck. It took a minute for the rocking of the boat to settle down and the three of them regained their feet.

"Bastard!" Captain Jack said as he dove back down the hatch in the wheelhouse. The humming sound had stopped.

"Did the pump stall?" Wayne asked Captain Jack as he climbed back out of the hatch.

"It did." Captain Jack said gritting his teeth. "But it does not matter. The bastard has sunk my boat."

Wayne and Wyatt looked at one another and then towards the shore. It wasn't a very long swim—-unless something was waiting in the water for you...

"Thoughts." Wayne said.

"To keep it off us long enough to get on shore." Wyatt said.

"Yes." Wayne said.

"What? We swim?" Captain Jack asked. "If that is a gator, one of us is not going to make it to shore."

"Your boat is sinking. We are going into that water whether we want to or not." Wayne said.

"If it's our friend the Gillman then what we need is that electric rod Ferguson had." Wyatt said. "It certainly intimidated the creature."

"Maybe...that's all we need." Wayne said.

"What do you mean?" Wyatt asked.

"Just the idea that might have an electric rod." Wayne turned to Captain Jack. "Your battery is inside the console isn't it?"

"Yeah." Captain Jack said.

"Pull it out. And a couple of cables attached to it that we can hold." Wayne said.

"We can't take that battery with us in the water." Wyatt said.

"No, but if we can generate some current, even a little in the water..." Wayne started.

"Our friend will sense it and keep his distance. Right most aquatic creatures can sense electric currents in the water." Wyatt nodded his approval.

"I am hoping it will buy us enough time to reach the shore." Wayne said.

"Hope so. And, if everything goes as usual, it's going to be close." Wyatt said.

Captain Jack emerged from the wheelhouse holding a battery with two cables attached to it.

"You get you battery ready." Wyatt said walking back down along the side of the boat.

"What are you going to do?" Wayne asked watching Wyatt.

Wyatt held up the rifle. "This won't do me any good in the water so I might as well get some use out of it now. I am going to keep him busy, if I can."

Wayne examined the battery as Wyatt began firing indiscriminately into the water all around the boat.

There was a shudder that ran through the boat and it settled noticeably lower in the water.

“My beautiful boat is soon to be at the bottom of the river.” Captain Jack said.

“OK.” Wayne said and pulled the battery over to the port side of the boat, on the opposite side they would be swimming from. “Let’s see if we can instill a little fear into whatever is down there.”

Wayne carefully lowered the terminals into the water. Some bubbles churned up to the surface, but no other obvious sign of anything showed. After a minute Wayne took it to the starboard side.

"Get ready. When I pull the terminals out we go." Wayne said. The other two nodded. Wayne dropped the terminals in and waited. Finally he pulled them out and nodded to Captain Jack and Wyatt.

Wyatt dove in followed by a reluctant Captain Jack. Wayne tossed the battery terminals aside and dove it as well. All three began swimming as fast as they could towards the shore.

Wayne glanced over at Wyatt. He saw the rifle slung on to Wyatt's back. "I thought that was going to be useless in here."

Wyatt looked over at Wayne. "It is and it's probably slowing me down some, but better to be eaten by an alligator than to incur another loss on the expense report."

"Right. Good thinking." Wayne said.

Wayne stopped swimming. He looked around one moment Wyatt was there and then he was gone. It was dark and Wayne was hoping he had just lost sight of Wyatt in the dark, but the lack of splashing told him that wasn't the case. He tried sticking his head underwater, but it was pitch black down there.

With a splash Wyatt broke the surface and sucked in a breath.

"What happened?" Wayne asked.

"Something grabbed my leg. Pulled me down." Wyatt said between breaths.

"What was it?" Wayne said as they both pushed on towards the shore.

"Don't know." Wyatt said. "I kicked it. Hit it somewhere with my foot and it let me go."

They reached the shore and climbed up on to the grassy embankment.

"That was lucky." Wayne said.

Wyatt sighed. "Yeah. Somehow, though, I don't think if it was an alligator it would have let go so easily. I don't think a kick in the snout would have deterred it."

"You think it was our friend?" Wayne asked.

"No sir, the gator would have dragged you to the bottom. Drowned you. That is what they do. Lazy bastards. Can't even bother to fight with you." Captain Jack said as he lay in the grass behind Wayne and Wyatt.

"I don't know if it was the Gillman or not. None of this behavior," Wyatt waved at the large swirl of bubbles that was all that remained of Captain Jack's boat, "seems like an alligator."

"If it was the creature we need a lot more manpower to cover a river this size." Wayne said.

"Agreed. This is his natural habitat. He can move at will in here." Wyatt said.

"I think we need to talk to the Director and see what he wants to do." Wayne said.

"Who is this Director man?" Captain Jack asked.

"He's our boss." Wyatt said.

"Well, tell him he owes me a boat." Captain Jack said.

Wayne looked over at Wyatt. "Accounting is going to love that."

11

"So, what's the plan?" Wyatt asked Wayne as he walked back out of the house and sat down in the grass along the river as the morning sun glinted off the water.

"What about my boat?" Captain Jack asked.

"You'll be paid for your boat. The government always pays it's debts." Wayne said.

Captain Jack shook his head. "No. No sir. The government never pays it's debts."

"That's not, well, OK, the government sometimes pays it's debts. Anyway, you'll get paid for your boat. You just have to fill out the proper forms." Wayne said.

"Forms. No. Forms are bad. They always give you forms instead of money. No. Forms are not good." Captain Jack shook his head emphatically. "Go back in. Tell your Director about the ex-wives."

"What ex-wives?" Wayne asked.

"My ex-wives. They need their money. My money. If you think your monsters are bad you should see my ex-wives. I need my money. I need my boat." Captain Jack said.

"We will talk about your money later." Wayne said.

"Yeah." Wyatt said to Captain Jack. "One national crisis at a time."

Wyatt looked over at Wayne. "So do we need another boat? Are they sending us some help?"

"Another boat! You will just wreck that one too." Captain Jack chimed in.

"Neither." Wayne said, ignoring Captain Jack.

"Neither?" Wyatt asked.

"Neither. The Director says this waterway runs all the way down to the Everglades. We're searching for a needle in a hay stack. We could be searching for the Gillman for a year and still might not catch him. He said he cannot tie up OSO resources like that." Wayne said.

"So, we're going to just let the Gillman roam free down here?" Wyatt asked.

"Well, the Director wanted to know if we knew for sure that the Gillman was still alive." Wayne said.

"You mean because we haven't seen him since the night the police were shooting at him? Do you really think that was an alligator attacking the boat last night?" Wyatt asked.

"I know, but we have no proof." Wayne said.

"Hah! Alligator. That has no alligator that sank my boat. They do not make alligators big enough to sink my beautiful boat." Captain Jack said.

Wyatt waved at Captain Jack. "What more proof do you need than the word of Captain Jack?"

Wayne sighed. "Yeah. If Captain Jack says it there's at least a 3% chance it's true."

"Yes sir. That is the truth." Captain Jack said nodding vigorously. "Wait. This 3 cents. This does not sound big. Is that big?"

"So is there a plan?" Wyatt asked.

"The Director has talked to Collins, the governor, and he is going to pull together some resources, local police, maybe some military and monitor the waterway. As much of it as they can. If they do spot him then they'll go after him, but, as far as we are concerned, well, we're done here." Wayne said.

They sat quietly for a moment.

"This kind of feels like a failure. We came down here to make sure this exact scenario didn't happen." Wyatt said.

"I know." Wayne said nodding. "But we did try to warn them at Ocean Harbor."

"Arrogant fools." Wyatt said disgustedly. "You can't control these kinds of creatures."

"Yeah." Wayne stood up. "Come on, Captain. Let's go find some forms for you to fill out and see if you can spell your name correctly."

Wyatt and Captain Jack stood up.

"Spell my name? Of course Captain Jack can spell his own name." Captain Jack said. A worried expression suddenly crossed his face. "Wait. If I spell my name wrong do I not get my money?"

K McConnell

From the case files of the
Office of Scientific Operations:

Declassified File

Public Release #3B

File #165

1955

Commonly referred to by the public as "It Came From Beneath The Sea"

1

Marcus Edmonds, the Director of the Office of Scientific Operations, a stocky man in his early fifties, set the receiver back down on the phone. He stared at the phone for a moment longer and then reached for the intercom.

"Jennifer?" Marcus asked.

"Yes sir?" Jennifer, Marcus' secretary answered.

"Have Elliot come into my office please." Marcus said.

"Yes sir." Jennifer replied.

Minutes later, after a brief knock on the door Elliot Simms, a District Chief Investigator for the OSO, entered.

"Sit down, Elliot." Marcus waved to the chair in front of his desk.

Simms sat down and pushed back his dark brown hair. He was the senior most investigator of the OSO agents.

"Trouble, sir?" Simms asked.

Marcus sighed. "Not sure. I've just had a call from Admiral Norman. I've known him for many years now and he is a no nonsense man. He's not one for jumping quickly into things."

"But the Navy has a problem?" Simms asked.

"They are puzzled. Are you familiar with the launching recently of the new atomic submarine?" Marcus asked.

"I read about it. More advanced than anything else in the world, isn't it?" Simms asked.

"Yes. Faster. More armored. It just returned to Pearl Harbor after it's initial shakedown in the Pacific." Marcus said.

"So...there's a problem?" Simms asked.

"The sub came back into port with some minor damage." Marcus said.

"I hadn't heard about that." Simms said.

"It's not public knowledge. The damage was...as I said, minor, but strange. And the circumstances that caused the damage were also...odd." Marcus said.

"Well, that sounds like our kind of thing." Simms said with a trace of a smile on his typically serious features.

Marcus nodded. "It does. That's why Admiral Norman decided to call me."

"So what made the incident odd?" Simms asked.

"The damage was to the stern diving plane. Apparently the sub encountered something on the return trip to Pearl and a piece of that *something* was caught in the diving plane." Marcus explained.

"What did the sub encounter?" Simms asked.

"They don't know. Whatever it was stopped the sub and held it in place." Marcus said.

Simms leaned forward slightly. "It *held* that sub in place? How is that possible? The only thing I could think of big enough to stop an atomic sub would be that creature we saw in Tokyo, but that thing is dead."

"I certainly hope so. That sounded worse than the Rhedosaurus was in New York. What did the Japanese call that thing?" Marcus asked.

"Uh, I think they referred to it as Godzilla." Simms said.

Marcus shook his head. "Unbelievable. Anyway, they don't know what it was that they encountered. All they know is that it had a hold of them and then they broke free, but it damaged the stern diving planes and left some organic material behind."

"What kind of organic material?" Simms asked.

"Don't know yet. They have a couple of experts working on it right now. A...doctor..." Marcus looked at some notes he had jotted down, "John Carter from Harvard and a doctor Lesley Joyce from the Southeastern Institute of Oceanography. They are both marine biologists."

"So, what's our plan?" Simms asked.

"I am thinking, in light of this business in Japan we need to take a look at this incident to make sure we don't have a similar problem of our own." Marcus said.

"Are you thinking another monster like that Godzilla thing?" Simms asked.

Marcus gave a small shrug. "I don't know. Maybe it's nothing, but, as you well know, we need to be proactive in these matters."

"Right, sir." Simms said.

"With that in mind I am sending you and agent Regan out to Pearl. Find out what this thing is that the sub encountered. You need to determine if this is something we need to be concerned about or not." Marcus said.

"OK. We'll leave immediately." Simms said standing up.

It took Simms and Regan almost 24 hours to get from Washington to Pearl Harbor. They were met at the airport by a jeep from the Naval base and driven to the shipyard where the organic material from the sub's stern diving plane was being studied. They pulled up and parked in front of a gray building with signs warning of radioactivity.

"Thank God we can get straight to work instead of, you know, getting some sleep." District Investigator Robbie Regan said as he slowly got out of the jeep.

"You slept on the plane." Simms said.

"You know how many times I've had to get a night's sleep on a bumpy plane ride." Regan asked, pushing back a lock of sandy blonde hair from his forehead.

"I really haven't been keeping track." Simms said.

"Somebody should be." Regan said as they walked into the building. The guards at the door saluted their escort, but ignored them.

Once inside the door there was a reception desk with a very serious looking soldier sitting behind it. He looked up at the three of them.

"This is OSO agent Simms and agent Regan." The sailor that had driven them from the airport informed the soldier at the desk and then immediately departed. Apparently that was all he had been tasked with.

The soldier sitting at the desk stared at Simms and Regan blankly. It was obvious he had no idea what he was supposed to do with them.

Before he could say anything a man turned a corner from a hallway further back and headed straight for the reception desk.

"I'll take care of them." The approaching man said. As he drew near it was clear he was a Naval officer.

"Gentlemen. I'm Commander Mathews." Mathews shook their hands.

"OSO District Chief Investigator Simms and this is DI Regan." Simms said.

"Admiral Norman called to inform me you two were coming out. Glad to see you. You're the monster hunting guys, right?" Mathews said.

"That's not technically our job description." Simms said.

"It's not far off though." Regan volunteered.

"Well, it's good to have you onboard. Don't know what this thing is, but they tell me it's big." Mathews said.

"That's what doctors Carter and Joyce say?" Simms asked.

Mathews nodded. "Yeah, but that's about all they can say at the moment."

“They haven’t identified the creature yet?” Simms asked.

Mathews shook his head. “No. My suspicions are they have an idea what it is, but just aren’t saying until they are 100 percent sure. You know how these egg heads are.”

“Ah, they’re the worst.” Regan said smiling.

Simms glanced over at him. He knew Regan was being sarcastic since Robbie Regan had graduated at the top of his class in Engineering at Cal Tech and had completed his Master’s degree before being recruited by the OSO. He also knew that Commander Mathews had no idea Regan was bullshitting him.

“Right. Well, let’s go in so you can meet them.” Mathews said gesturing back down the hall.

They walked back down the central main hall and then turned left down another long hall. About half way down this hall they stopped just outside a door.

Mathews pointed to a red light above the door. “Check that before you go in. If it’s on then they have something radioactive out and you have to wait. Believe me, you don’t want to just blunder in. Doctor Joyce can be...well, a little vocal if you forget to check that.”

“Right.” Simms said. “Check the light.”

“Well, I would think the radioactivity would be something of a deterrent too.” Regan said.

Mathews gesture was something between a nod and a shrug. “You would think, but it turns out Doctor Joyce seems, somehow, more dangerous.” Mathews gave a mischievous smile.

"We'll bear that in mind." Regan said.

They went into the lab and wove their way through several long tables covered in chemistry equipment. A dark haired woman and a taller man were each focused on individual tasks. The woman was closely examining the contents of a test tube, while the man was busy focusing a microscope.

"Doctor Joyce, this is agents Simms and Regan. From the OSO." Mathews said smiling at Joyce.

Lesley Joyce glanced at Simms and Regan. She looked back at the test tube. "I've never heard of the OSO. I thought this was a top secret facility."

Mathews cleared his throat a little. "Uh, the OSO, the Office of Scientific Operations actually has higher clearances than we do."

Joyce stopped staring at the test tube and looked at Simms and Regan again. "Oh. Well what is it you guys do?"

"The OSO?" The tall man said pulling himself away from the microscope. He took a step closer to them and extended his hand. "John Carter."

Simms shook Carter's hand and Regan did as well.

"DCI Simms and this is DI Regan. The OSO is familiar with your work. Very impressive." Simms said.

"Well, it's a pleasure to finally meet someone from the OSO. I have heard about you guys. You're the monster hunters." Carter said with a whimsical smile.

"Well..." Simms started.

"Yeah, that's us." Regan said.

"Monster hunters?" Joyce asked.

"Yes, these are the guys that show up when there's big trouble." Carter said. "Were you guys involved at all in that business in Tokyo?"

Simms nodded. "We...had a limited role in that."

"Wow, I would really love to hear about that." Carter said.

"A story for another time." Mathews said. "Right now we just have to determine if there is big trouble here."

"Right. Of course." Carter said.

"But...monster hunters?" Joyce repeated.

"Yes, you heard about that prehistoric creature in New York a couple of years ago. What did they call that thing?" Carter asked.

"A Rhedosaurus." Regan volunteered.

"Yes, that was it." Carter said.

"They caused that?" Joyce asked.

"No. They were involved in destroying that thing. Well, both creatures. You guys worked with my cousin." Mathews said.

"Your cousin?" Regan asked.

"Yeah, Colonel Evans." Mathews said.

"Ah, yes. Good man." Simms said.

"Yeah, it kind of runs in the family. We have another cousin in the Air Force, Captain Pat Hendry." Mathews said proudly.

Simms thought for a moment. "Wasn't he involved with that incident in the Arctic a few years ago?"

Mathews nodded. "That was him. Not sure what it was all about. Something to do with little green men I think, but the Air Force squelched the whole story later on. It's all classified now."

"Seems like your family's a magnet for this kind of trouble." Regan said.

Mathews nodded slightly and glanced over at the table full of experiments that Carter and Joyce were working on. "Yeah, well, I was hoping I could avoid that fate."

"Well, we should let you get back to work." Simms said. "The sooner you can identify what we're dealing with the sooner we can come up with a plan for what can be done about it."

Mathews escorted Simms and Regan back out of the building. They spent the next hour getting settled into a barracks and getting badges that would allow them to move freely around the base since most of the base personnel would have no idea who or what the OSO was.

2

Simms and Regan walked into the Commissary the following morning and made straight for the coffee maker. They each drew a cup of coffee. Simms waved a hand towards a table where Carter and Joyce were already sitting.

"May we join you?" Simms asked as they walked up to the table.

"Certainly." Carter said waving at unoccupied chairs.

Simms and Regan sat down.

"So Doctor Carter I wanted to ask you if, in your opinion, you thought this specimen you are working on could have come from a prehistoric creature?" Simms asked.

"Prehistoric?" Carter shook his head. "No. The cellular structure we are looking at is from a contemporary species. I am certain of that. Afraid it is one of your dinosaurs from the past?" Carter asked with a smile.

Simms smiled slightly with a shrug. "Just checking."

"It's kind of a standard question for us." Regan said.

"This is a marine species of some kind. Just bigger than expected. It will be a fascinating discovery once we find it." Lesley Joyce said.

"Perhaps." Simms said. "Not all newly discovered species take kindly to humans studying them."

"I suppose you guys will just want to kill it." Joyce said.

"Now Lesley..." Carter said.

"If it is determined to be a threat to people then we might recommend that. Generally, the military makes that call." Simms replied.

"Well, we know what they will want to do." Joyce said flatly.

"I understand your interest in studying this thing, Doctor Joyce, but it is the job of the OSO and the military to protect the people of the United States. If this thing turns out to be a threat to people then we are obligated to negate that threat in whatever way necessary." Simms said.

“He’s right.” Carter said. “I want to study this thing as much as anyone, but the safety of the public can’t be sacrificed in the process.”

Lesley shrugged. “I know. It’s just that this is the find of a lifetime.”

“Yours or mine?” Regan asked.

Lesley glanced over at Regan. Her expression at first was puzzled and then, realizing what the OSO had dealt with in the past understood what he meant.

"Well, we should probably get back to it." Carter said standing up. Lesley stood up too and with a wave they headed out of the Commissary.

Later, while Simms and Regan were in another barracks Mathews appeared at the door. He waved for them to follow him out.

"What's up Captain?" Regan asked.

"They think they figured out what it was." Mathews said.

All three stood silent for a moment.

"So...do we need to show you our credentials again or what?" Regan asked.

"Oh, sorry. I was going to let them explain it to you. I find it a little hard to believe. Climb in." Mathews waved towards the jeep sitting beside the door of the barracks.

Mathews drove them over to the lab and led them in.

"So," Mathews said indicating Simms and Regan, "tell them your theory."

"It's not a theory." Carter said.

"You said it was a theory." Mathews said confused.

"Well, it was when you left, but it's not now." Lesley said.

"Theory or not, maybe you could just tell us." Simms said.

"Right." Carter said. "Octopus Vulgaris."

"An octopus." Simms said.

"The squishy things with tentacles?" Regan asked.

"Not exactly the scientific definition, but yes." Carter said.

"An octopus big enough to stop an atomic submarine?" Simms asked.

"Yes." Carter said.

"Since when do we have octopus that big?" Simms asked.

"Don't know." Carter answered. "But there's no doubt. It's Vulgaris."

"Why haven't we seen these things before?" Regan asked.

Carter shrugged. "I can't answer that either."

Simms looked over at Mathews. "And the Navy hasn't encountered anything like this before?"

Mathews shook his head. "Not that I've ever heard of."

"That suggests that there aren't lots of these things running around out there." Simms said.

“Possibly.” Mathews agreed with a nod.

“Doesn’t tell us anything about it’s origins, though.” Simms said. “Is it possible this is somehow related to atomic testing in the Pacific?”

Carter nodded. “We were discussing that very thought just before you arrived, though not in the way I suspect you are thinking.”

“I am thinking about the creature that attacked Tokyo recently. The Japanese think that our atomic testing may have created that creature, though our scientists are highly skeptical of that theory. We at the OSO have to keep an open mind about such things so we cannot dismiss the possibility.” Simms said.

“I know that’s what you were thinking.” Carter said. He shook his head. “I don’t think this creature was created by any atomic testing. We think this creature was simply driven out of it’s natural habitat in the deep ocean by fallout from the atomic testing.”

“How would atomic blasts on a Pacific island reach all the way down to the ocean bottom?” Regan asked.

“We think the creature has a mild dose of radioactivity that is warning it’s potential prey that it’s approaching and this has forced the creature to seek other nontraditional prey outside of it’s normal habitat.” Lesley explained.

"So it's moved out of the deep ocean and closer to the surface?" Simms asked.

"Exactly." Carter answered.

"You heard about how part of the Japanese fishing fleet disappeared recently, right?" Lesley asked.

Simms nodded. "We were aware of that. We were monitoring that situation."

"Because you thought it might be another creature like the one that showed up in Tokyo?" Carter asked.

"Yes." Simms answered.

"Well, we are thinking that missing fishing fleet may be the work of Captain Mathews' creature." Carter said.

Mathews waved a hand. "Oh, no. It's not my creature. I just happened to bump into it."

"OK, so if we assume then that this creature is not a product of atomic testing like the Japanese think their Godzilla creature was then can you tell me the general vicinity you believe this creature is from?" Simms asked.

Carter glanced at Joyce. "We believe it have originated in Mindanao Deep."

Simms hesitated. "Is that near the islands of Indonesia?"

Carter shook his head. "No. It would be north of that. Close to the Philippines."

"Can you show me?" Simms said waving towards the large map of the Pacific behind them.

Lesley stepped over to the map as they all turned around. "Right in this general area." She circled a finger around just east of the Philippines.

Simms stared at the map for a minute.

"You're thinking about Zeitner's island." Regan said to Simms.

Simms nodded. "Just curious."

"What is Zeitner's island?" Lesley asked.

Simms waved off the question. "Nothing. I don't think it's related to this."

A sailor came into the lab and saluted Captain Mathews. "Sir, the admirals are here."

Mathews returned the salute. He looked at the rest of them. "I'll go escort our distinguished guests in." He left the lab with the sailor.

Simms pulled Regan aside. "Let's stay inconspicuously out of the way of this. I would rather not answer any questions concerning this. The undersecretary of the Navy was going to be here as well and I believe he doesn't think highly of the OSO."

Regan nodded. "Agreed."

Simms and Regan stood back and watched Carter and Joyce present their findings and theories to Admirals Burns and Norman and the undersecretary of the Navy. It quickly became obvious that the admirals and the undersecretary were hesitant to embrace the idea of a giant octopus roaming the Pacific and attacking whole ships. When the meeting was finished there was clear frustration on the part of both Carter and Joyce. It did not seem that any immediate or significant action was going to happen.

As Captain Mathews left the lab following the meeting Simms and Regan caught up with him.

"The meeting didn't seem to go as well as you might have hoped." Simms suggested.

"Uh, sorry, things on my mind." Mathews waved a hand towards his head.

"I was just saying that didn't seem like the admirals were convinced this creature really exists." Simms said.

"Oh, that. Well, sometimes it's hard to read what an admiral is thinking." Mathews said.

"Well, I just want to let you know that regardless of what the Navy thinks about the existence of this creature the OSO considers this a serious matter and will give you any support we can in dealing with it." Simms told Mathews.

Mathews stopped and looked at Simms. "Support me? In dealing with it?"

"Yes." Simms said.

Mathews shook his head. "I'm not doing anything until the Admiralty decides what to do. Then I'll do whatever I'm ordered to do. That's how we do things in the Navy."

"Right." Simms said. "We will continue to investigate the matter and as soon as you do receive orders to do something, we will be at your disposal to help."

"Sorry." Mathews said. "As I said, things on my mind. Anyway, I appreciate your help in all this." With a nod Mathews strode away.

Simms and Regan stood in the hall of the lab for a moment longer.

"You sure there's going to be something for us to do here?" Regan asked.

Simms nodded. "I am. I definitely think something's out there. Don't you?"

"Absolutely. Not so much because of the evidence, but because, as our luck would have it..." Regan said.

"Yeah. Well, there is that too." Simms agreed.

3

The following morning Simms and Regan stopped by the Naval base Communication building. With no current leads on the whereabouts of the creature they had decided to sift through the various reports that filtered through the Naval communications chatter.

"Hey Jimmy." Regan said as he and Simms entered the primary radio room.

"Hey, Mr. Regan." The sailor said sliding one side of his headphones off his ear as he looked up from the panel lights, switches and phone jacks in front of him.

"Anything interesting?" Regan asked.

"Ah, just the usual stuff." Jimmy said with a wave towards a pile of papers to his left.

Regan looked at Simms. "Well, should we just split the pile up and sift through them?"

Simms nodded. "Yeah. Guess that's the best way to get through them."

"Oh, wait." Jimmy turned to the pile and shuffled through it. "There was one...here it is. I thought you might find this interesting." He pulled a sheet of paper with some hand writing on it and handed it to Regan.

Regan read it. "Hmm, a missing yacht." He handed the paper to Simms.

Simms read the report. "That's what? 60 miles east of Pearl?"

Regan nodded. "Sounds like it."

"We could take a plane out there and check that out." Simms said.

"Yeah. Might be nothing, but it's better than sitting around here waiting for something to happen."

"Agreed." Simms said.

With a little help from Captain Mathews the base commander provided a seaplane and a pilot for Simms and Regan to use for the day.

After prepping the plane they lifted off from Pearl Harbor and headed east to the last known location of the missing yacht. It took them about 40 minutes to reach the area at which point they started slowly circling in wider and wider arcs searching for any sign of the yacht.

"What's that?" Regan pointed into the distance from the window on his side of the plane.

"Where?" Simms leaned around Regan to look through his binoculars out the window. "Ah, yeah. That looks like something." Simms tapped the pilot on the shoulder and pointed.

With a nod from the pilot the plane banked around. As it approached the spot the pilot dropped the plane down closer to the sea.

At this altitude as they passed over the area they could see what was obviously the shattered remnants of a boat.

"Not much left of that, assuming it was a boat to start with." Regan said.

"It looks like boat debris. Crushed boat debris." Simms said.

"Not sure anyone could have survived that." Regan commented.

"Over here." Simms said pointing out his side of the plane. Regan leaned over and spotted a larger piece of wreckage that someone seemed to be clinging to.

"Can you land or is it too choppy?" Simms asked the pilot.

The pilot shrugged. "I've landed in worse." He swung the plane around so he was better oriented in relation to the waves. He brought the plane down and after a couple of stomach churning skips the plane eased to a stop on to the waves and bobbed up and down.

Simms and Regan climbed out on to the pontoon of the plane. They held on tightly as the waves bounced the plane up and down. They were still about 30 feet from the piece of wreckage.

"Well, I guess I could swim over to it." Regan said staring over at what looked like a section of the hull with a prone figure draped on top of it.

"Wait." Simms said pointing. There were several dark shapes moving only a few feet beneath the surface.

"Sharks. Nice." Regan said. "Any ideas?"

"Don't get eaten." Simms said.

"Sound advice." Regan said. "Maybe you could explain that to the sharks."

"We need something to keep the sharks occupied." Simms said.

"Well, what interests a shark?" Regan asked.

"Food." Simms said drawing his .45 out. He took aim at a passing shark and fired.

"Ah. That might work." Regan pulled out his gun and started firing at the same shark. Fortunately the shark was close enough to the surface they were able to wound it. A moment later the wounded shark was quickly moving off. Several other dark shadows veered off in pursuit of the wounded shark.

Simms leaned into the plane and called out to the pilot. "Can you get us any closer?"

The pilot shook his head. "Can't risk that debris puncturing the floats."

"Oh well." Regan said pulling his jacket and shoulder holster off. He handed them to Simms. "Toss me a line when I get over there."

Simms nodded. He set Regan's jacket and holster in the plane and rummaged around for a rope.

Regan dove into the water and swam over to the section of boat hull. He ducked his head under the water a couple of times to check for sharks, but didn't see any. When he reached the piece of debris he was forced to work his way around to the far side of it in order to climb up on to it. Pulling himself up, Regan shuffled over to the prone figure. From the air he had thought it was a man clinging to the boat, but now that he was kneeling next to the person he realized it was a woman. The young woman was wearing blue jeans, a black and white checkered shirt with the sleeves rolled up and flat deck shoes. She was blonde and

Regan thought she was somewhere in her mid twenties. Her eyes were closed and she looked like she was suffering from some exposure from the hot sun and dehydration.

"Catch this rope!" Simms yelled over to Regan. Regan waved and Simms threw the rope. It took three tries for Regan to get a hold of it.

"Tie the rope around you and I will pull you and him over here." Simms called out.

"Her." Regan answered.

"What?" Simms asked.

"He's a her." Regan said.

Simms and Regan stared at each other for a moment. Simms waved a hand. "I don't care. Just tie the rope around you."

Regan got the rope tied around his waist. He was studying how best to grab the woman when something caught his attention. He turned and noticed another dark shape swimming past the bobbing debris he was kneeling on.

"Hey!" Regan got Simms' attention and pointed at the shadow as it passed.

"Great." Simms said loud enough for Regan to hear. "I'm guessing they are all over the place here now."

Regan nodded. "Well, pull fast."

Simms nodded. "Agreed." Simms turned to the pilot still inside the plane cabin. "You're going to need to pull too."

The pilot hesitated.

"Now would be the time for you to get your ass out of that seat and in the door here to help pull." Simms said, making it clear it was an order.

The pilot hesitated for another second, but he knew these two men were somebody important and had a feeling he might be mopping floors by nightfall if he didn't comply. A quick scramble later and he was sitting in the door holding part of the rope.

Simms nodded to Regan who, holding the woman around the waist, nodded back. With a shove Regan pushed off the wooden piece of debris and Simms and the pilot began pulling on the rope as fast as possible.

Regan kicked to keep both his head and the woman's head above water. He was only partially successful at it. At one point his kick solidly hit something that felt thick and alive. A moment later Regan saw a dark shadow close in on them. He stopped kicking to keep his head above the water and sank slightly below the surface. He saw the shark moving in for what looked like an attack. Regan pulled his legs in. As soon as the shark was nearly on him Regan kicked with both legs. He hit the shark dead on the end of it's snout. In a flash the shark veered left and disappeared.

A hand grabbed Regan's shoulder and he looked up to see Simms kneeling down on the pontoon. An instant later Simms let go and Regan slid back completely into the water. Two shots rang out above Regan's head and then Simms' hands were again pulling at Regan and the woman. A third hand, the pilot's, helped pull them up on to the plane's float.

The pilot climbed back into his seat to make room. Simms backed into the plane as Regan pushed the woman into the backseat of the plane. Regan climbed in and closed the door.

"Well, that was fun." Regan said.

"I am sensing sarcasm there, but I don't know what you are complaining about. It's not like there was a giant octopus out there." Simms said with a smile.

"Monsters or not, they weren't very friendly out there." Regan said.

The woman, now slouching between them in the cramped backseat, groaned. Regan found some water and slowly poured it into her mouth. It took a few minutes, but she seemed to be recovering a little. Her eyes flickered and then opened.

"Where am I?" She asked as the pilot started picking up some speed for takeoff.

"You're aboard a seaplane." Regan said.

"How...how did I get here?" The woman asked.

"We pulled you off a piece of wreckage." Regan said.

"Do you remember what happened to you?" Simms asked the woman.

She looked confused.

"What's your name?" Regan asked.

"Rebecca. Rebecca Woods." The woman answered.

"I am Robbie Regan and this is Elliot Simms. We are from the OSO. We're here to help you. Do you remember what happened to you?" Regan asked.

Rebecca Woods stared at Regan for a moment, focusing on him. "What's an OSO?"

"Well, it's the Office of Scientific Operations, but that's not important. Rebecca, can you remember what happened to the boat you were on?" Regan asked again.

"Beka."

"What?" Regan asked.

"My friends call me Beka." The woman answered.

"OK, Beka, but the boat...?" Regan persisted.

Beka seemed confused for a moment and then her eyes grew wider. "Oh my God. The boat. It just...exploded."

"There was an explosion?" Simms asked.

Beka glanced at Simms and shook her head. "No. I don't think so. It was more like it just shattered."

Regan looked over at Simms and then back to Beka. "You mean the boat was crushed by something?"

"That's what it seemed like." Beka looked up at Regan. "What could cause a thing like that?"

"You didn't see what happened?" Regan asked.

Beka shook her head. "No. It happened at night. We were all sleeping."

"We'll get you back to Pearl Harbor." Simms said.

"Did you find any other people?" Beka asked.

"We didn't see anyone else. I'm sorry." Regan said.

Beka didn't seem to react to Regan's words.

"Did you...lose someone from the boat?" Regan asked.

Simms gave Regan a questioning look. He didn't see how that was a relevant question.

Beka shook her head. "I didn't really know them very well. A friend of a friend you might say. They were just going out for a fun cruise. A couple of days of fishing and sun. That's all."

"So you said the boat seemed to shatter. Was it like you hit something?" Simms asked.

Beka shook her head. "No. More like something hit us, but from two sides."

"Two sides?" Regan asked.

"Yeah. It was hot out and I was sleeping out on the deck. Near the front." Beka said.

"The bow." Simms said.

"The what?" Beka asked.

"The bow. The front of a vessel is called the bow." Simms said.

"Really? A nautical lesson right now?" Regan asked looking at Simms.

Simms waved it off. "Never mind. OK, you were near the...front. Then what?"

"The whole boat shook and then there was something big and black around the middle of the boat and there was a crashing sound and the boat was in pieces." Beka said.

"What did the black thing look like?" Regan asked.

Beka shook her head. "I don't know. It was dark."

"Sounds like our friend." Regan said looking at Simms.

Simms nodded slightly. "Could be."

"What do you mean a friend of yours?" Beka asked.

Regan shrugged a little. "Nothing."

"Do you know what wrecked that boat?" Beka asked.

"Maybe. We're not sure." Regan answered.

"Well what was it?" Beka asked.

"We think it was a monster." Regan said.

Beka stared at Regan for a moment. "Well, if you don't want to tell me you could have just said so."

"I did tell you." Regan said.

"A monster. And you expect me to believe that our boat was attacked by a monster?" Beka asked.

"We think so." Regan replied.

"A monster?" Beka asked.

"Yes, ma'am." Regan answered.

"First, don't call me ma'am. My name is Beka. Second, who goes around looking for monsters?" Beka asked.

"We do. It's kind of our job." Regan said.

"Your job? What kind of job is that?" Beka asked.

"It's the Office of Scientific Operations. It's what we do." Regan said.

"Well, that sounds like a stupid job if you ask me." Beka said.

Regan nodded slightly. "Sometimes, Beka, it kind of is."

4

"What do you think Director?" Admiral Norman asked as he sat in his office. He had been struggling to determine a course of action. On the one hand if all these events turned out to just be a series of coincidences then he would look like a fool for sounding an alarm about a giant octopus roaming around the Pacific. On the other hand, if this creature was really out there and he did nothing to try to stop it, well he wouldn't be an admiral much longer.

"Admiral," Marcus said, "I can't tell you what to do, but I can tell you that my men say this threat is real. I trust them. They are experienced in this kind of situation. Their instincts are good. If they say it's real, then I think we have to take it seriously."

Admiral Norman sighed. "I think, for whatever reason, I felt the same way, but I just didn't want to believe it. Where do these things keep coming from?"

"I don't know. We are trying very hard here at the OSO to determine if there is a common source for the increase in these kinds of events. Unfortunately, we haven't been able to definitively find a single source that is causing it." Marcus said.

"Well, I guess I have no choice with this latest ship sinking between Vancouver and Honolulu, but to put the Navy on high alert." Admiral Norman said.

"I think that's a good first step, but I think you will need to go beyond that." Marcus said.

"What are you thinking?" Admiral Norman asked.

"Well, I think you are going to need to restrict all maritime traffic in at least the northern Pacific." Marcus said.

"All maritime traffic? The only way I could do that is full fledged blockade of the Pacific shipping channels. I would have dozens of nations screaming at us." Admiral Norman said.

"I understand that, but it is the only way to limit the casualties. As long as all these easy targets are out there for this creature it will feed off them indefinitely." Marcus replied.

Admiral Norman was silent for a minute. "I will have to talk to the President about this. We risk starting a war stopping all shipping in the Pacific. Our adversaries will claim it is an excuse to seize control of the Pacific."

"Maybe, but if we can convince them we are doing it to protect their interests we might get some assistance from them." Marcus said.

"I highly doubt the Soviets will see it that way." Admiral Norman let out a long weary sigh. "I will talk to Ike and see what he says. I appreciate your input, Marcus. I know your opinion will go a long way in convincing the President we need to do this."

"I will direct my men to do whatever they need to do in order to get solid proof that this creature is real and it is the cause of this string of maritime disasters." Marcus said. He said goodbye and hung up.

Marcus sat for a couple of minutes staring down at his desk. It was going to be a thorny task to try to stop Pacific shipping, find a giant monster, kill it and not start a war.

"Jennifer." Marcus spoke into the intercom.

"Yes sir." Jennifer replied.

"Track down Elliot. I need to talk to him." Marcus told her.

"Right away, sir." Jennifer replied.

As their seaplane came to a stop and taxied over to a hangar a sailor pulled up in a jeep. As soon as Simms, Regan and Beka had climbed out of the plane the sailor came over to them.

"Agent Simms?" The sailor looked at Regan.

Regan pointed over at Simms. "That guy."

The sailor turned to Simms. "Agent Simms your office is trying to reach you."

Simms nodded. "Can you get me to an office with a phone?"

The sailor waved towards the jeep. "Yes sir."

"Coming?" Simms asked Regan.

Regan glanced at Beka. "Go ahead. I'll catch up."

Simms nodded and the jeep drove off.

Regan looked at Beka. "So, I can arrange for a jeep to take you somewhere."

Beka glanced across the airfield. "Something's going on, isn't it?"

Regan hesitated. Normally he would just send a civilian like her off the base, telling her as little as possible and get on with his assignment, but from the moment he pulled her off the piece of wreckage Regan had an odd feeling that this woman was different than most. For the first time in this job he was somewhat conflicted about the need to keep the civilian population at arm's length.

"Well, I'm not really at liberty to say." Regan said. It sounded just as lame when he said it as it had in his head.

"So, you guys are some secret government agents or something?" Beka asked.

"Something like that." Regan said.

"What did you call it? The OOS?" Beka asked.

"The OSO." Regan answered. "Is there somewhere I can take you to?"

"What does that stand for? Overly Secret Oddballs?" Beka said a smile.

Regan smiled. "Sometimes, I think. It's the Office of Scientific Operations."

"Ah, that sounds more governmental. So what exactly do you guys do?" Beka asked.

"Well, we look for trouble." Regan said.

"What kind of trouble?" Beka asked.

"You are very curious." Regan eyed her suspiciously.

Beka caught his look and shrugged. "Sorry. My father was in the OSS in the war. He tended to be curious and suspicious of almost everything. I think it was an occupational hazard. I also think he passed that on to me."

"Ah, guess that makes sense." Regan nodded.

"So what kind of trouble do you guys look for. Oh, wait. You said monsters. Really?" Beka persisted.

"Monsters." Regan said, watching her reaction.

Beka studied Regan for a moment. She seemed to be deciding if he was just bullshitting her or not.

"You're serious." Beka said.

Regan nodded slowly. "Yeah."

Beka was quiet for a moment. "I thought you were joking before. You mean monsters like that thing they said was in Tokyo?"

Regan nodded. "Yes. Actually, we were there. Just observing. Mostly anyway."

"Wow." That's all Beka could say.

"So, as I said, I can arrange to have you dropped off somewhere in Pearl if you want." Regan said.

"Do you think a monster attacked the boat I was on?" Beka asked.

"Possibly." Regan said. "Clearly something big struck that boat."

Beka seemed to be thinking back on that night and she shuddered slightly. "That's for sure."

Regan was going to say something and then stopped. He stared at Beka for a moment. "You don't have anywhere to go, do you?"

Beka looked at Regan. She hesitated and then shook her head slightly. "No. Not really. I've...been drifting a bit recently. Running away, really. Long story. Personal things. Anyway, I met a girl in San Francisco. She was coming out here. She had some family here and invited me to come along, on a whim. So I came."

"She was on the boat?" Regan asked.

Beka nodded.

Regan sighed. He stared out across the tarmac for a moment. “OK. Well, let’s go see what Elliot has heard from our boss and then we’ll figure out what to do with you.”

“Elliot?” Beka asked.

“Agent Simms.” Regan said.

“Oh, right.” Beka thought for a moment. “If I remember correctly, you had a first name too.”

“Robbie.” Regan said.

“Robbie. That’s a nice name.” Beka said with a smile.

“Good.” Regan said. “It’s the only one I’ve got.”

5

"You're still here." Simms said looking at Beka.

"I'm still here." Beka replied.

"She had nowhere to go." Regan said in answer to Simms' questioning look.

"Well, we do." Simms said.

"Where is the Director sending us?" Regan asked.

"The Director isn't sending us anywhere. I volunteered us to investigate a problem off the coast of Canada with Doctor Carter." Simms said.

"So we're going to Canada?" Beka asked.

Regan and Simms looked at Beka.

"You're not going to Canada." Simms said flatly.

"You know I've never been to Canada." Beka said.

"Not relevant." Simms said.

"So what did the Director have to say?" Regan asked.

"He wants us to come up with some kind of hard evidence for this creature as soon as possible. There are big decisions being made with significant consequences—-namely a Naval blockade of the Pacific." Simms said.

"Hmm, I doubt that will be well received. There's bound to be a lot of countries screaming about that." Regan said.

"Yes, so time is of the essence." Simms said.

"So when do we leave?" Beka asked.

Regan and Simms looked at Beka, again.

"You can't just throw me out on to the street." Beka said.

"Can't we just say she is a witness to the creature and stow her in one of the barracks?" Regan asked.

"I will *not* be *stowed* somewhere." Beka said.

Simms sighed. He ran a hand across his face. "I don't imagine the base commander is going to want a civilian wandering the base right now."

"So, again, when do we leave?" Beka asked.

"Ma'am—-" Simms stopped when he saw the look in Beka's eyes. "I mean, Miss Beka, I don't think you realize exactly what we do."

"You hunt monsters." Beka said.

Simms looked at Regan.

Regan shrugged. "Well, she asked."

"Well, *you* do not hunt monsters." Simms said.

"My father did. In the OSS. A different kind of monster." Beka said.

"That may be true, but it hardly qualifies you for this." Simms turned to Regan. "And why aren't you saying anything?"

"Because," Regan said with a shrug, "I think it's easier fighting monsters."

The small transport plane left the air base carrying the four of them. They sat in the back in the seats along the fuselage facing inward. Regan and Beka sat on one side and Simms and Carter were opposite them on the other.

Carter leaned over so Simms could hear him better. "So, why is the woman coming along with us?"

"We got tired of arguing with her." Simms said.

Carter nodded. "Say no more. I totally understand."

They were in flight for about an hour and a half when the plane began banking right. It seemed an odd maneuver because they assumed their flight to Vancouver would be a straight shot. Simms glanced at Regan who looked a little puzzled as well.

The curtain separating the cockpit from them flapped open.

"Doctor Carter!" The copilot yelled.

"Yes?" Carter called out.

The copilot waved for him to come forward. "Urgent message for you."

Carter unbuckled himself and moved carefully up to the cockpit. After a couple of minutes he returned.

"What is it?" Simms asked.

“Captain Mathews and Lesley have found something on the coast of Oregon. They want me there. We are diverting to Portland and then you guys can go from there up to Vancouver and the weather station.” Carter answered.

Simms nodded. He looked at Regan and pointed to Carter. “Oregon.” Simms called out.

Regan nodded.

"What's going on?" Beka asked.

"It seems Doctor Carter has been redirected to Oregon." Regan said.

"Why?" Beka asked.

Regan shook his head. "Don't know."

They touched down in Portland where a car was waiting for Carter. A short time later they were in the air again. In Vancouver they switched to a seaplane and headed northwest. After a while they saw the thick forests of Vancouver Island give way to a choppy ocean. Finally the plane descended and, after a couple of passes to gauge the waves just offshore of a small island, the pilot, Eddie, brought the plane in for a jolting landing. It was a rough taxi to the dock as well.

"Sorry about that people." Eddie said. He was a jittery middle age guy that desperately needed a shave and a haircut of his jet black hair. "I think there's a storm moving in from the west. It's making things a little choppy around here."

From the dock the four of them, Simms, Regan, Beka and Eddie took in the rocky little island. There was an old lighthouse and a stone cabin next to it. A rough built and somewhat damaged wooden shed stood a short distance from the cabin. There was a small stone wall built along one side of the island presumably to help keep the sea at bay in rough weather that now seemed to have partially crumbled.

What seemed to draw everyone's attention the most was the remains of a radio tower that now lay in pieces on the ground. A line of bent metal sections were lying all about.

As the four of them approached the cabin three guys came out the door of the cabin. They seemed to be in something of a hurry as they met the visitors.

"Thank God you're here. We didn't realize somebody was coming out to get us." The first man said. He was a man in his early fifties, partially gray hair and thin beard.

"Uh, well, I'm not sure..." Simms was thinking about the fact that the seaplane probably couldn't accommodate all seven of them.

"Oh, I'm being rude. I am Evan Bruley. Meteorologist. Western Canadian District." He held his hand out and shook Simms'.

"And this," Bruley said turning to the two younger men next to him, "is Jimmy Wheatley from UCLA and Benton Quest from CalTech. They are doing internships with me up here."

Wheatley was taller with light brown hair and dressed in expensive sport clothes. Quest was red haired and dressed in a casual button down shirt and jeans.

"Agent Simms and Agent Regan from the Office of Scientific Operations. From the States." Simms said.

"Office of..." Bruley started slowly.

"Office of Scientific Operations." Quest said quietly. "I have heard of you guys."

"Really?" Regan said. "That's rare."

"Hi, I'm Beka." Beka said stepping forward and shaking their hands.

"Oh, are you with the Office of Science...whatever too?" Bruley said smiling at Beka.

"No. She's not." Simms answered quickly.

"I'm just helping them out." Beka said with a smile.

"No. She's not." Simms repeated.

"Yes I am." Beka said still smiling.

"She's more like an observer." Regan said.

"No. She's not." Simms continued.

"A helping observer." Beka said.

"Well...OK." Bruley said clearly unsure what was going on.

"So, what's this about us coming to get you?" Regan asked.

Bruley looked oddly at them for a moment. "Yes. Didn't you come out here to get us. I sent out a message on the radio. Well, I think I got the message out before the tower went down."

Simms shook his head. "No. The Canadian authorities indicated they haven't heard from you and couldn't raise you on the radio."

"Yeah. That thing took down the tower." Wheatley said.

Simms and Regan glanced at one another.

"What thing?" Simms asked.

"The tentacle thing." Wheatley answered.

"Some kind of cephalopod. But very large." Quest volunteered.

"Well, I guess we came to the right place." Regan said.

"No. You don't understand." Bruley said. "We need to get off this island as fast as possible. That thing has destroyed the radio tower, it smashed part of the shed and even tore down some of the sea wall. It's only a matter of time before it tears everything down and us with it."

"Well we are here to—-" A loud screeching sound interrupted Simms. Everyone turned towards the sound and saw a slimy tentacle wrapped around the plane. Under the weight and strength of the tentacle the plane was crumpling and the metal was making an awful racket as it was crushed.

In an instant Simms and Regan were racing back down to the dock. They had their guns drawn and were firing at the tentacle. By the time they got down to the dock the plane was mostly submerged about ten feet out from the dock. It was obvious the plane would never fly again. It was also obvious that the bullets from the two .45s that Simms and Regan always carried had little effect on the creature. It was simply too big to be bothered by bullets.

"My plane! My plane!" Eddie cried.

Simms and Regan stared out at the water for a couple more minutes, but the creature did not reappear. They walked back up to the others.

"So much for escaping this place." Wheatley said dejectedly.

"We'll figure something out. We're not beaten yet." Quest said.

"You...ran after that thing." Beka said slowly.

Regan looked at her. "Yeah. We kind of needed that plane."

"Yeah, but...it was huge. I mean...really huge." Beka said.

Regan shrugged. "Yeah, well, it's what we do."

"That's crazy shit." Wheatley said.

"Let's all go inside and see what our options are." Simms said.

They filed into the cabin. It had a small kitchen part, a coal stove, a table and four chairs and a couple of bunk beds. A couple of oil lamps dimly lit the room.

"So, what are the odds we could get enough of the radio tower up to get the radio working again?" Simms asked looking at the three residents of the island.

"I...don't think that's possible." Bruley said.

"What he means is the radio had very poor reception with the full tower up. It's unlikely with anything less than the full tower it would pull anything in. It's a pretty old model. The transmission and reception circuits are ill suited for this place." Quest said.

Simms looked at Quest and nodded. This guy is pretty smart, he thought.

"The plane." Regan said looking at Eddie. "It has a radio. A better radio than this one." He waved towards the old radio that sat on a small table in the corner.

"But...my plane is wrecked. It's sunk." Eddie said sadly shaking his head.

"We'd have to dive into it and yank it out of there." Simms said looking at Regan.

"Right. A cold swim, but doable." Regan said.

"What? You're going jump into that water? With that monster out there?" Beka said. She looked at Regan.

Regan shrugged, but didn't say anything.

"You think if we got that radio and got at least some of that tower back up we might be able to make contact with Vancouver Island?" Simms directed his question to Quest.

Benton Quest thought for a moment and then nodded. "I think it might work. It's worth a try."

"Seriously? Jump in freezing cold water with a monster to get a radio?" Beka asked, still looking at Regan.

"We need the radio." Regan said. For some reason he didn't understand he reached out and put a hand on her shoulder.

Beka sighed. "How can I help?"

Simms wanted to say something, but decided against it.

"Can you shoot a gun?" Regan asked.

"Damn straight." Beka said.

Regan smiled. "Good. You can watch for the monster."

"You're going to have the girl watch for the monster?" Eddie asked.

"Beka and the creature are old friends." Regan said smiling at Beka.

"I guess so." Beka said.

"She won't be alone." Simms said looking at Eddie. "You're going to have my gun."

"What? Go down by the water with that thing out there? No way." Eddie said.

"It's your plane." Regan said.

"Actually, it belongs to the Seattle Air Freight Company." Eddie said. It was obvious that somehow he thought that would get him out of the assignment.

Simms and Regan exchanged a smile.

"Perfect. An American company." Simms said.

"What does that mean?" Eddie looked a little uneasy.

"It means," Regan said, "we have the authority to requisition you and your plane for anything we deem necessary."

"What? Who says?" Eddie said.

"President Eisenhower." Simms said. "Our authority comes directly from him."

"Seriously?" Beka asked.

Regan nodded. "Yeah."

"Whoa." Bruley commented.

"You're bullshitting me." Eddie said.

"I don't think so." Quest said. "I'm pretty sure the OSO has that kind of authority."

Everyone was quiet for a moment and, with the exception of Simms and Regan, they all seemed to now view the two OSO agents in a different light.

"What the hell is the OSO?" Eddie asked.

"Can you shoot a gun?" Simms asked. He held up his .45.

Eddie hesitated. "Yeah. I can shoot it."

"It's getting dark." Regan said glancing at the small window. "A storm is coming and the day is getting late."

"Yeah." Simms said. "We'll have to make our dive in the morning."

“I guess we could offer you some coffee.” Bruley said walking over to the small kitchen area. “It’s about all we have left. We were supposed to be picked up two days ago.”

Beka looked around. “I hate to ask this, but I don’t see a bathroom.”

“It’s out by the generator shed.” Wheatley said waving towards the door.

“Out? You mean like an outhouse?” Beka asked.

“Yeah. Afraid so.” Bruley said.

“So, I have to sit over a smelly hole and hope a giant sea creature doesn’t kill me? Wonderful.” Beka said

“I’ll go out there with you. I mean, not in the...you know. I’ll just...” Regan said.

"You're hired." Beka said and, waving Regan to follow her, they walked out the door of the cabin.

"Thank you." Beka said as the two of them walked across towards the generator shed.

"Well, I don't think any of us should be out here alone right now." Regan said looking off towards the ocean.

"Yeah, well no one should have to face an outhouse alone, but I meant about trusting me to guard you guys when you go down for the radio." Beka said.

Regan wasn't sure what to say. He didn't know why he trusted Beka, but for some reason he did. Maybe because she had survived hours clinging to a piece of wreckage from a boat crushed by a massive sea creature and surrounded by sharks and seemed hardly disturbed by the whole incident. It was a characteristic that Regan had rarely seen, except in the OSO.

"Yeah, well, I don't know. I..." Regan stumbled along.

Beka put a hand on Regan's shoulder, pulled him a little closer and kissed him on the cheek. "Anyway, thank you."

"Sure." Regan said taking up a position outside the well aged door of the outhouse as Beka ventured in. Regan's thoughts seemed to bounce around some. This was a very strange twist to their typical assignments.

A wave crashed into the sea wall on the far side of the cabin. It made a roaring sound and Regan almost jumped. His mind had been elsewhere and suddenly he realized he still had a job to do. He slid his .45 out of it's shoulder holster and his eyes swept around the small island. He wasn't sure what he could really do with a .45 against that creature, but he wasn't going to worry about that right now.

"Well, that was an adventure." Beka said emerging from the outhouse.

"I think I'd rather not hear the details of that." Regan said.

"Probably not. So, no Mrs. Regan anxiously waiting back home somewhere?" Beka asked.

Regan shook his head. "No. Our job doesn't really lend itself to wives, families, white picket fences, those kinds of things."

"Yeah. I guess I could see that. 'Honey, I'm heading out now to go slay some dragons. Give the kids hugs and kisses.'" Beka said with a laugh.

"My preference is to have the Army slay the dragons. I prefer to just point them in the right direction." Regan said.

"Is that how it usually goes?" Beka asked.

Regan shook his head. "No. Not usually. Typically we end up running and shooting a lot."

"So what you need is a woman that understands what you do. Someone that is independent and not sitting by the window at home wringing her hands." Beka said smiling at Regan.

Regan took a deep breath and let it out slowly. "Uh..."

Beka laughed. "Come on. Let's get back into the cabin and out of this wind."

"So why don't we just go into the lighthouse? It's higher up from the water than this cabin?" Eddie was asking as Regan and Beka walked in.

"That lighthouse is an empty shell. They haven't used that for many years now. These days only the light at the top which runs off the generator is still in use." Bruley answered.

"Still it's high up." Eddie insisted.

"Structurally I doubt it is any safer. Probably less." Quest said.

A gust of wind and the slap of rain struck the side of the cabin as the storm announced it's arrival. Wheatley found some crackers in one of the kitchen cabinets and passed them around to everyone for a meager dinner of crackers and coffee.

They all sat around and talked quietly for a little while until Simms suddenly held up a hand for everyone to be quiet. They all sat silently for a moment.

"Something?" Regan asked.

Simms glanced at Regan. "More like a feeling. A vibration."

"There." Quest said.

"Right." Simms agreed. He slid his gun out. Regan did the same. With a nod they moved towards the door.

"Robbie?" Beka said watching Regan. She had stood up.

Regan held up a hand for her to stay put. There was a definite ground shake now and everyone stood up. Simms eased the door open and the sound of the wind and rain became magnified.

Simms and Regan stepped out into the storm. They looked around, but didn't see anything unusual, though their visibility was somewhat limited. A vibration accompanied by a grating noise came from the far side of the cabin. They moved to the corner of the cabin and stared at the old lighthouse. There were two thick black bands wrapped around it.

"What the hell is it doing?" Regan asked.

"I think it's trying to pull it down." Simms said.

"That's pretty damned close to the cabin." Regan said.

"Yeah." Simms agreed. They both ran back to the door of the cabin.

Simms stuck his head in the door. "Everyone out!"

Moments later the group stood outside between the generator shed and the cabin as the old lighthouse buckled under the pressure from the creatures tentacles. A segment of the top part of the lighthouse grazed the cabin shearing off a piece of the stone corner. A three foot gap now at the top corner of the cabin now allowed rain to sweep into the cabin's interior.

With the lighthouse destroyed the tentacles slid back into the sea.

"You know those damned things are a beacon for these monsters." Regan said.

“Does seem like that.” Simms said.

They waited for a few minutes more, but no other sign of the creature was seen. They walked back into the cabin and inspected the hole in the cabin wall.

“I don’t supposed there are any tarps laying around here.” Simms said.

“I think there’s some old sail cloth in the generator shed.” Bruley said.

“That would probably at least keep the rain and some of the wind out.” Simms said.

“We can go grab it.” Quest said gesturing towards Wheatley.

“Me?” Wheatley asked.

“It’s just rain out there.” Quest said.

“And that creature.” Wheatley said.

“Yeah, well, it seems to prefer buildings.” Quest pointed out.

Wheatley stared at Quest for a moment.

“And you’re standing in a building.” Quest continued.

Wheatley thought for a moment more. “Oh, OK, I guess.”

They went out into the storm to retrieve the sail cloth.

"What do you think?" Regan asked Simms quietly as they stood by the door. Beka stood next to Regan listening.

"I think it would be nice if we had more weapons." Simms said.

"Can't argue with that." Regan agreed.

"You think we are in real trouble here?" Beka said, her voice sounded a little shaky.

Regan shrugged. "We have been in far worse situations than this." He smiled at Beka.

Simms watched Regan and Beka for a moment. This was definitely a new wrinkle to things. There was no OSO rule against having personal relationships, but there was an almost universal unspoken understanding that it was best not to be distracted by personal matters in their line of work. A moment's hesitation because your mind was elsewhere could be the difference between life and death. Still, they weren't machines.

Regan looked over at Simms. There was something in his look that Simms had never seen before. Regan seemed to be asking him for help with something. It took Simms another moment to get it.

"Right. Yeah. We have been in much worse predicaments than this. We'll figure something out." Simms said.

Beka looked back and forth at the two of them. "You know you two are terrible liars, right?"

"Is bullshitting different than lying?" Regan asked.

"I think it is." Simms said.

"OK, then we might be bad liars but...well, anyway, the truth is we have been in a lot of tough situations, but, it's part of what we do. As Elliot said, we'll figure something out." Regan said.

"Oddly, that is kind of comforting." Beka said.

Wheatley and Quest lumbered through the door wrestling a roll of heavy canvas. Eddie and Bruley joined the two young men in hoisting the sail over the corner of the building to keep the rain and wind out while Simms and Regan kept watch for the creature. Bruley stoked up the coal stove while the rest of them pulled their wet coats off once they were back in the cabin.

“So, I think we should come up with a plan for defending this place.” Simms said as they all found a place to sit and nurse a cup of coffee.

“How are we gonna do that? You guys are the only ones with guns.” Eddie said.

“And those don’t seem to have much effect on the creature.” Simms agreed nodding.

“Well, there you go.” Wheatley said shaking his head. “We’re doomed.”

“You have an idea?” Quest asked Simms.

"I was thinking maybe we could use that generator to keep the creature from tearing this place down." Simms waved around the cabin. "If we could wrap cables around the building and tie them into the generator then when the creature tries to grab this cabin we could give it quite a jolt."

"That would be a nice surprise for it." Bruley said.

Simms glanced at Quest and saw he was thinking it over.

Finally Quest spoke up. "I'm not sure of the feasibility of that."

"Don't be so negative." Wheatley said. "It's our only chance."

"What are you thinking?" Simms asked Quest.

"Not sure we have enough cables here to go around the cabin and we would have to get them high enough off the ground to prevent them from just shorting out into the ground. I don't think in this storm we could run cable high up on the cabin." Quest said.

Simms sighed. "You may be right."

"But..." Quest started and then stopped, still thinking.

"Go ahead." Simms said encouragingly.

"Well, I believe it has been shown that all creatures give off a certain level of electromagnetic energy." Quest said.

"Right. That's what Lesley was saying." Regan nodded, glancing over at Simms.

"Who's Lesley?" Beka eyed Regan.

"Doctor Joyce. Back in Pearl." Regan said.

"Right." Simms agreed. "That's how the creature searches for food."

"I am wondering if the creature is sensing electromagnetic energy here and is searching for it." Quest said.

"You mean like us?" Bruley asked.

Quest shook his head. "I am doubtful it could sense us very well if we weren't in the water. I think it would have to be something stronger than our tiny energy fields."

"The generator." Simms said.

"Yes." Quest said.

"So we just give the generator to the creature and we are safe?" Wheatley asked. "Let's do it."

"Without the generator..." Regan started.

Simms nodded. "Right. Getting the radio out of the plane wouldn't do us any good. No power to send a signal. We would still be stuck here."

"We would need a battery in lieu of the generator." Regan said.

"Isn't there a battery in the plane?" Bruley asked.

Eddie frowned. "There is, but...it's kind of a bitch to get at. Don't know how you would get it out diving down in cold dark water. Besides, I think the salt water would have drained it by now."

"If we had the battery, though," Quest said, "we could recharge it from the generator before we send it out."

"Send it out?" Bruley asked.

"I was thinking if we sent generator out on a raft of some kind the creature would find the magnets in it appealing. It would probably ignore us after that." Quest explained.

Simms thought for a moment. "Not a bad idea."

"So you're saying we gotta get the battery and the radio out of a sunken plane, charge the battery up some way from the generator, then build a raft to hold the generator and send it out to sea and hope the creature follows that instead of coming after us?" Wheatley asked.

"Seems simple enough." Regan said with a smile.

"Doesn't sound that simple." Eddie commented.

"You haven't seen some of our past plans." Regan said.

"Hey, you're supposed to be comforting." Beka said.

"Sorry." Regan said.

Simms glanced at his watch. "We've got about 4 hours until sunrise so we should get whatever sleep we can. We have a lot of work to get done in the morning."

6

Morning found the group sipping coffee with no one getting much sleep. Without saying anything they all gathered in the middle of the cabin.

"Agent Regan, Beka, Eddie and myself will go down to the dock and begin the retrieval of the radio and the battery. We're going to need a raft for the generator and probably will need to try to get as much antenna back as possible." Simms looked at Bruley while he talked about the raft and the antenna.

"Right." Bruley said. "We can work on that." He glanced at Quest who nodded in return and got a shrug from Wheatley.

When they reached the dock Simms and Regan handed their guns over to Beka and Eddie. In return Eddie handed them a screw driver and a pair of pliers.

"Are you sure about this?" Beka asked Regan.

"You mean about you handling the gun?" Regan asked.

"No. About going down there?" Beka pointed at the tip of the wing of the plane that stuck out of the water. The wind had died down some and the waves were not as bad on this side of the island, but the cold water did not look inviting.

"I'm sure about it, but that's not the same as being happy about it." Regan said with a smile. He peeled off his jacket and shirt. He was still wearing a t-shirt. Simms followed suit. They walked to the end of the dock. They had already gone through with Eddie exactly how the radio would have to be pulled out. They would focus on the battery after getting the radio.

"Well?" Regan asked looking at Simms.

"After you." Simms replied.

They dove in and quickly disappeared into dark water. Beka and Eddie watched the ocean around them. Long minutes passed and the two resurfaced. They drew in air and dove back under. They surfaced again after a shorter period of time. After their third dive they swam back over and climbed back up on to the dock. Immediately Beka and Eddie wrapped blankets around them.

Simms handed Eddie the radio. "Check it over. See if it still looks OK." He spoke with chattering teeth.

Beka wrapped the blanket and herself around Regan. "You're freezing."

Simms and Eddie both looked at Beka and Regan. Eddie gave Simms an apprehensive look.

Simms shook his head at Eddie. "Don't even think about it."

"Good. Because I wasn't." Eddie said with a note of relief.

While Beka rubbed Regan's back and chest to help him warm up Simms went through with Eddie how they would have to get the battery out. They went through it a couple of times.

After some jumping around to try their best to generate some heat Simms and Regan indicated they were ready to go back in. They took a couple of deep breaths and in one motion dove back in.

Again, Beka and Eddie watched the mildly choppy water for any sign of the creature, but nothing appeared. There was a moment when Beka pointed out at the water having seen something break the surface, but after another moment several back humps indicated a pod of killer whales were passing the island.

This time it took five dives to get the battery and both Simms and Regan needed help getting back on to the dock. They were both exhausted and in the early stages of hypothermia, but they had the battery.

Eddie and Beka had to help Simms and Regan stumble back up to the cabin where they sat down next to the coal stove. It took them more than a half hour to feel something close to normal again.

Bruley came in to check on them and tell them they had erected about 15 feet of antenna and the younger guys were making good progress on a raft for the generator. He thought they would be able to launch it soon.

"As soon as Benton is available Eddie could use his help in getting the radio back in working order and the battery charged." Simms said.

"I can get the radio working if I can get some DC current for it." Eddie said.

Bruley nodded. "I'll see what Benton can do about that. I'll help Wheatley finish up the raft."

Before anyone could move there was scream and everyone ran for the door of the cabin. Outside was a chaotic mess around the generator shed. Next to the shed they had been attaching wood and buoys to the sides of the generator. Now the generator shed was a pile of rubble and a tentacle still lingered on top of the pile.

"James!" Bruley yelled as all of them ran towards the chaos.

They caught a glimpse of Wheatley wrapped in a tentacle and being pulled into the waves breaking against the rocky shore. Another tentacle had the generator with it's partially attached outrigging and was dragging that into the water as well. Off to one side Benton Quest was still rolling on the ground away from another tentacle as it probed around the ground for anything else of interest.

While everyone else quickly slowed their pace as they drew closer to the creatures wavering tentacles, Simms and Regan moved much closer. With guns drawn they began firing at the tentacles, in particular the one searching for Quest.

"Not getting much satisfaction from this." Regan said.

"I agree." Simms acknowledged. "Let's concentrate on a single spot."

"It would be easier if the damned thing would stop moving." Regan said.

"Right in this general area." Simms said firing into a section of the tentacle.

Regan focused on that area as well and the creature, after several more shots, pulled the tentacle back down into the water.

"Empty." Regan said as he reloaded.

"Me too." Simms said flipping the empty cartridge out and jamming another in.

"That's a lot of bullets just to sting it." Regan said.

"Yeah." Simms said as they crossed over to Quest and helped him up.

"You OK?" Simms asked Quest.

"Yeah. Wheatley?" Quest asked.

"Gone." Regan answered. "We should probably retreat back from the water. Not sure that thing is going to be completely satisfied with the generator."

They watched, as they backed up, the generator slowly disappear into the waves firmly gripped in a tentacle. The other tentacles had also sunk back into the water.

Regan felt a hand on his back. He glanced around.

"You got really close to that thing." Beka said, her voice was almost scolding.

"Yeah. I often get a front row seat to these things." Regan said. "Comes with the job."

"You're job sucks." Eddie said.

"Yeah, well, the benefits are great though." Regan said.

"Really?" Eddie asked.

"No." Regan said shaking his head.

"We didn't get the battery charged." Simms said staring out at where the generator disappeared.

"So...we need to hope there is still some kind of charge left in the battery." Bruley said.

"It's possible there's enough for a short message." Quest said.

"We only need one short message to get help." Simms said.

"But...we may not know if we were heard." Quest pointed out.

"Well, let's send the signal first and worry about everything else later." Simms said.

While Eddie and Benton Quest worked on getting the radio, the battery and the antenna hooked up Simms and Regan wandered around the outside of the cabin keeping an eye out for the creature's return. When Beka leaned out the door of the cabin to tell them the radio was ready Simms and Regan headed back in without seeing any sign of the creature.

"So how much time do you think we have before what's left in the battery runs out?" Simms asked Quest.

Quest shrugged. "Not sure. No easy way to test it without running it down. Based on some preliminary tests with the equipment I would guess about five minutes. Maybe ten. At most."

"Plenty of time." Simms said.

"As long as someone at the Department of Marine and Fisheries is listening." Bruley said.

"Well, fortunately we're not calling the Canadian government." Simms said with a slight smile.

"Who are we calling?" Bruley asked.

"The United States government." Simms said.

"Who in the United States government would be listening for something on a low radio band way out here?" Eddie asked.

"You'd be surprised." Regan said.

That's why you wanted us to wait before attempting to contact anyone until you were here." Bruley said.

"Yes." Simms said.

Simms told Quest what frequency to set the radio to. "So, are we ready?"

Quest nodded and with a nod from Simms he switched on the radio.

Simms picked up the mic. "XZ9377. XZ9377."

Simms released the button on the mic. A moment passed.

"Acknowledged." A voice came over the radio.

Everyone except Simms and Regan looked at one another.

"E-X-T. E-X-T. Q6. Q6." Simms said into the mic. Another moment passed.

"Acknowledged." The voice replied.

"Who is that?" Bruley asked.

"Uncle Sam." Regan said with a smile.

"The coordinates." Simms said to Quest who handed him a piece of paper.

Simms read the longitude and latitude of their location. He read it twice.

"Acknowledged and confirmed." The voice answered.

"Clear." Simms said into the mic.

"Clear." The voice replied.

"That's it?" Eddie asked.

"That's it." Simms said.

"What happens now?" Bruley asked.

"We wait." Regan said.

"For what?" Bruley pressed.

"Depends on who's closest." Regan said.

"What does that mean?" Eddie asked.

"If there are any Navy ships nearby they'll come here. Otherwise it will probably be a seaplane." Simms said.

"Hope it's bigger than mine was. There's six of us." Eddie said.

"They know how many of us there are." Simms said.

"How...?" Bruley asked.

"Oh, the Q6 thing." Beka said.

Regan smiled at her. "Yes. We'll make an agent of you yet."

"No. We won't." Simms said.

"Are there any women OSO agents?" Beka asked.

"No. There aren't." Simms said definitively.

"Why not?" Beka asked.

"Because women don't take no for an answer." Simms said.

"Well I could be the first." Beka said.

"No. You won't." Simms said.

"Would I have to live in Washington DC? I don't think I would like it there. Maybe I could live somewhere else and you guys could just pick me up on the way to somewhere." Beka said. She smiled at Simms.

Simms sighed. "Is there any coffee left?"

Three hours later a seaplane banked around and landed near the dock. It was large enough to hold all six of them and though they all watched the ocean below as they gained altitude there had still been no further sign of the creature.

7

"Well, look what the cephalopod dragged in." Carter said as a corporal escorted Simms, Regan and Beka into the large open office area of the Operations Division of the 12th Naval District offices. Carter sat at a desk sipping a cup of coffee.

"I heard something about your little adventure with our friend." Carter said.

"Yeah, well we wanted to tire it out a little before it came to see you in Oregon." Regan replied.

"Ah, you heard about that. Yes, the creature seems to be working it's way down the Pacific coast hunting for food. It seemed to be picking it's way along grabbing anything or anyone off beaches or the shoreline whenever the opportunity presented itself. We've ordered people to stay away from the coast." Carter said.

"So, what's the situation here?" Simms asked.

"We have developed a new weapon we think will destroy the creature if we can get a shot at it. I am about to go out on patrol along the coast." Carter said.

"What's this new weapon?" Simms asked.

"Actually," Carter glanced at his watch, "I need to get down to the airfield, but Lesley will be down here in a little while with the Admiral to explain what we're doing to the press. She can tell you all about it."

"Alright." Simms said. "Happy hunting."

A short time later Lesley walked into the large office leading Admiral Burns and some men from the press. She gave a quick look in their direction and then led everyone over to a large wall map of the west coast of the United States.

The Admiral spoke about what was currently being done to protect the city of San Francisco and the bay area which involved a submarine net capable of holding an electric charge being stretched across the mouth of the bay. Then Lesley called Carter on a radio as he was flying on patrol. He explained to the men from the press the plan to use this new weapon to almost instantly destroy the creature in lieu of indiscriminately bombing it.

"So are we going with them?" Beka asked as the press guys, Lesley and the Admiral headed out to go down to the docks and see the new weapon.

"*All* of us are not going down there." Simms said.

"Why aren't you going?" Beka said. "I'm curious to see this new weapon thing."

"*I* am going." Simms said.

"Well, that doesn't make any sense. Robbie should see the thing too." Beka said.

"He is." Simms said exasperated. "You're not going."

"Don't be silly." Beka said with a wave as she started walking towards the door. "Hurry up or you guys will miss it."

Simms looked at Regan. "You need to talk to her. She can't just come with us."

"Yeah, well, you've seen how effective it is telling what she will or won't be doing." Regan said.

"Come on, Robbie. You know sooner or later we are going to be in a really tight spot." Simms said.

Regan nodded. "I know. I'll talk to her."

They rode on down to the dock and hover a short distance away from the rest as Lesley and Admiral Burns explained how the new weapon, a modified torpedo, was designed to stick into the creature with a harpoon and then be detonated remotely to be certain that the creature was hit.

"OK, so you've seen this new weapon, now will you please go to the hotel and wait there?" Regan said to Beka.

Simms had drifted closer to the group of journalists to listen some more.

"Not until after you feed me some lunch. I'm starving. Where did you say this hotel was?" Beka asked.

"It's in Sausilito. Across the Golden Gate bridge." Regan said.

The group of reporters broke up and headed away from the docks. Lesley told Simms that she and Captain Mathews were going back to the 12 Naval District headquarters to monitor the situation. Simms told her they would catch up with her in a little while.

"So, what's our plan?" Simms asked looking at Regan.

"Lunch. Then Beka has agreed to some rest at a hotel over in Sausilito." Regan said.

Simms looked at Beka. She shrugged.

"I'll go, but only as a favor to Robbie." Beka said.

"OK. I guess I am kind of hungry too." Simms said with a nod.

After a lunch in the shadow of the Golden Gate bridge they crossed the bridge and made their way into Sausilito. They zigzagged around a little to find the quaint little seaside hotel and stood at the desk getting Beka checked in. While Beka was signing the register explosions could be heard in the distance.

Simms and Regan looked at one another.

"Let's go." Simms said.

"Maybe I should..." Beka started.

Regan turned to her. "No. I need you to stay here."

Beka was about to say something, but instead she just looked into Regan's eyes. A moment passed.

"OK." Beka said. "I...should probably wash my hair before facing any monsters anyway."

"Thank you." Regan said.

There were more explosions from somewhere out towards the ocean.

"We have to go." Simms said.

"Right." Regan said still looking at Beka. She kissed him on the cheek.

"Be careful." Beka said.

"Always." Regan said with a smile.

Simms and Regan climbed back into the car.

Simms looked at Regan. "Since when are you *always* careful?"

Regan shrugged. "Since just now, I guess. It's a new thing I'm trying."

"That's not the only new thing you're trying." Simms said and started the car. They made their way through the streets of Sausilito and up to the Golden Gate bridge. A police car blocked traffic from getting on to the bridge.

Simms and Regan got out of the car and walked up to the police officer.

"What's going on?" Simms asked.

The policeman held up a hand. "No one can go out on the bridge. That sea creature thing is attacking it."

Simms and Regan moved to the railing of the bridge and looked down along it.

"There. At the far support." Regan pointed.

Simms leaned a little further out. "It looks like it is trying to pull itself up out of the water."

"Or pull the bridge down." Regan replied.

They could see several abandoned cars still out on the bridge. The creature had reached up was now pulling a section of the bridge down. The bridge lurched every time the creature pulled at it.

"There's still people out there." Regan said pointing.

Simms stared. "Some guy out towards the middle and...a car driving out towards him. It looks like Carter."

"And someone in that car right there." Regan pointed towards a car closer to their end of the bridge.

As they watched a woman and a child staggered out of the car. The instability of the bridge made walked difficult and they kept falling down.

"Come on." Simms said and the two of them were about to run out on to the bridge.

"Hold on. No one goes out there." The policeman got in front of them.

Simms whipped out his credentials. The policeman glanced at it. He was clearly puzzled at what it was or what it meant. Simms waved the policeman off and they pushed past him. The policeman hesitated while watching them run out on to the bridge and then, with a shrug, turned back to the group of people in front of him watching the events unfold.

They raced out towards the woman and child now crawling along the pavement, but even before they reached the woman the bridge seemed to settle down. They could see in the distance the creature's tentacles slide back down out of sight.

"Are you OK?" Simms asked the woman as he and Regan helped her and her son stand back up.

"I...I think so." The woman said hesitantly.

Simms brushed off her coat as they stood there. At first she seemed to be looking right at Simms and then past him. Her eyes grew big and she screamed.

Simms spun around to see a tentacle rising up above the railing of the bridge. A shot rang out. Regan had already pulled out his gun and fired at the tentacle.

"Too far away." Simms said as he drew his gun out.

"Go." Regan said to the woman pushing her towards the end of the bridge.

"What do you think?" Regan asked Simms.

"I think we need to buy a few minutes for the woman to get off the bridge before our friend here pulls this end down too." Simms said.

"Right." Regan said. He held up his .45. "With these?"

Simms nodded. "Work with what you have. I think we need to get next to that thing," Simms pointed at the tentacle as it started descending towards the bridge, "without getting crushed by it and focus on one spot. Like we did on the island."

Regan sighed. “This ought to be fun.” They watched the tentacle come down on the roadway making sure they were off to the side of it in the direction of the end of the bridge. When the tentacle came down the bridge shook and both of them stumbled.

Once back on their feet Simms pointed at a spot along the tentacle and they began firing into it. By the time they had emptied their clips the tentacle twitched some and then lifted back up off the pavement. They stood watching the tentacle rise up about ten feet above the pavement.

They assumed the tentacle was retreating back over the side of the bridge, but a moment later it was obvious they were wrong. The tentacle began moving towards them. It was trying to find what was stinging it. They dove backwards as the tentacle came down again right where they had been standing. Seconds later they were back on their feet and running now back towards the end of the bridge. If the tentacle came down again a little further to the left it would have easily crushed them, but a glance back told them the creature was pulling back off the bridge again.

They made it to the end of the bridge where the woman and her son stood with the policeman and the rest of the people.

“Thank you.” The woman said. “Thank you so much.”

Simms flashed a quick smile at her and patted her shoulder. Simms and Regan watched the tentacle completely disappear. They looked at the battered bridge.

“Looks like we are going to be taking the long way back around to the city.” Regan said.

“Looks like it.” Simms agreed.

8

Simms and Regan walked into the headquarters of the 12th Naval District. It had been an exhausting drive back around into Sausilito, Richmond and through Oakland to get back into San Francisco. The roads, especially the Bay bridge, were clogged with people trying to get out of San Francisco and the bay area in general.

As they walked into the communications center they saw Lesley and Carter standing at the far end of the big room. Simms had only walked a short distance into the room before he stopped and turned towards one of the many sailors manning phones at a long row of desks.

Regan nearly collided into Simms' back. "What's up?"

Simms leaned over to one of the sailors as he hung up a phone. "What was that message? Something about Hawaii?"

The sailor glanced up at Simms. He seemed to vaguely recognize him as somebody important. "Yes sir." He handed the piece of paper he had written the message down on to Simms.

Simms glanced at it. "Damn. I was afraid of that."

"What is it?" Regan asked.

"There's been a freighter, Chinese, attacked off of Hawaii." Simms said.

"When was that?" Regan asked.

"About 6 hours ago." Simms said.

"Hmm, that creature might be fast, but there's no way he could have gotten from Hawaii to here in 6 hours." Regan said.

"Exactly." Simms said.

"So...a second one." Regan said.

"Looks like it." Simms said. "Let's talk to our resident scientists about this."

"Where have you guys been? We've had some excitement here." Carter said as Simms and Regan walked up.

"We saw it. Along with you dancing about on a crumbling bridge." Regan said.

“Where were you?” Carter asked.

“We were on the far side of the bridge.” Simms said.

“What were you doing over there?” Carter looked at them.

Simms waved off the question and handed Carter the piece of paper.

Carter read it and looked at Simms grimly.

“What is it, John?” Lesley asked.

“Another attack.” Carter handed the paper to Lesley.

“Hawaii?” Lesley looked up from the paper confused.

“Are we sure it wasn’t just an accident of some kind?” Carter asked.

“No.” Simms said. “Which is why I think we should have the survivors of the ship interviewed. Let’s see what they have to say.”

Carter nodded. “I agree. I’ll arrange for that immediately.” He turned and headed to a phone on one of the desks.

“When the guys from the press asked you if there could be more of these things you said you probably.” Simms said to Lesley.

Lesley gave a weary nod. “I guess I was half expecting this, but I was truly hoping I was wrong.”

“Well, one thing at a time. Let’s get rid of this one before we go after the next.” Simms said.

"You're right." Lesley said with a certain resignation.

"Also," Simms said, "I was wondering, this creature, it's a giant octopus, right?"

Lesley nodded. "Yes."

"It can't function on land, correct?" Simms asked.

Lesley shook her head slowly. "No. It could briefly fully emerge from the water, but it couldn't last very long out of the water."

"Even a giant octopus that's been irradiated?" Simms asked.

Lesley hesitated. "Well, I suppose, given it's size, it could store more oxygen than a normal octopus which might give it a longer period of time out of the water, but it still wouldn't be able to venture very far from the ocean."

Simms gave a short nod. "OK. I just wanted to get a sense of what resources we might need if it turned out this thing could move around on land."

Carter rejoined them. "Naval Intelligence is going to interview the Chinese sailors they fished out of the water."

"Good." Simms said. "If this creature were blown to pieces would the...guts and blood be dangerous? Because of the radiation."

Carter nodded. "It could be. That's why we wanted to use the special torpedo and destroy it's internal organs. The torpedo will kill it without a big mess."

"Right." Simms said.

"You guys look exhausted." Carter said. "Why don't you get something to eat and some rest. We're just going to be monitoring the situation from here until the creature reappears."

"Well, a cup of coffee probably wouldn't hurt." Simms said. Simms and Regan walked back across the large office area towards the door. There was a lounge area just down the hall where there was always coffee brewing and sometimes sandwiches were brought in for the staff managing the phones and teletype machines.

Simms and Regan sat down at a table in the lounge. They each had a cup of coffee and Regan slowly inspected a sandwich.

"Are you going to eat that or question it?" Simms asked.

"I will probably pose one question to it and if it answers me, I'm not eating it." Regan said.

Simms stared down into his coffee.

"Something is on your mind." Regan commented.

"Suppose the Doctor Joyce is wrong. Suppose that thing can move on land." Simms said.

"Then I guess we bring in some heavy weapons and blast it back into the sea." Regan said.

"Even if the radioactive fallout makes part of the city uninhabitable?" Simms asked.

Regan shrugged. "The creature has to be stopped. The consequences of stopping it will have to be dealt with later."

Simms nodded. "I know. Sometimes I really understand the weight of the decisions that Marcus has to make. Determining how much collateral damage is acceptable. The problem is that collateral damage is typically people. Decisions you and I make affect the people we trying to help. For good or bad."

Regan didn't answer. He immediately thought about Beka.

"You're thinking about her, aren't you?" Simms asked.

Regan shrugged. "Yeah. I guess."

"This isn't a job that lends itself to relationships." Simms said.

"I know." Regan said.

They could hear some excitement in the other room. They got up and hurried into the command center. The phones were ringing everywhere.

"What's happening?" Simms asked Captain Mathews who was staring at the map.

"The creature has surfaced. It's down by Market Street and the docks." Mathews said.

Simms looked at Regan. "I think we need to observe this thing up close. We need to make sure it is limited to the shoreline."

Regan nodded. They told Captain Mathews they were headed down to the dock area and left the building. They knew the plan was for Mathews and his submarine to approach the creature from the sea and implant the special torpedo at point blank range.

Outside they commandeered a taxi and had the driver weave his way through the crowded streets as close as he could to Market Street. Simms and Regan abandoned the cab and worked the rest of the way to the waterfront on foot.

"Can't see much of it from here." Simms said standing in the street as panicked people streamed past.

"Well, I can tell you it's tearing that clock tower building down." Regan said pointing as two of the creature's tentacles pulled the top of the clock tower down.

"Yeah, but we need to see if it's actually emerging from the water." Simms said. "Come on."

Simms ran up to the corner of the block. Regan followed, but as they rounded the corner they immediately stopped.

"Holy Shit." Regan said. A tentacle was reaching up the street. They flattened themselves against a storefront as the tentacle came down crushing a group of people beneath it.

"Come on. We need to keep going." Simms said as he ran along the street keeping against the building as they moved parallel to the tentacle. They came up to a waterfront warehouse. It had large open doors that were used for delivery trucks.

"This way." Simms said and ducked to the right and into the warehouse.

As they crossed an open area used for loading there was a thundering sound from above them. They stopped and looked up. There was nothing to see but roof.

"There." Regan pointed towards windows high up on the wall facing the water. Through the windows they could see a tentacle. The building shook and small debris began falling from the roof down all around them.

"It's wrapped a tentacle over the building." Simms said. "We need to get out of here before the whole place comes down on us."

"Wait." Regan said grabbing Simms' arm. "Over there." He pointed at a corner of the loading area. There was a group of dock workers huddle behind some crates.

"Damn." Simms said. They started running over to the dock workers. The building shuddered and some of the support beams holding up the roof began buckling and falling.

Regan grabbed the back of Simms' jacket and yanked him backwards. A second later, where Simms had been, an I-beam crashed into the concrete.

"Thanks." Simms said. "That might have hurt."

"Very likely." Regan agreed.

“Let’s get these guys out of here.” Simms said climbing over the I-beam.

Regan followed Simms and they scrambled back into the corner where five guys were hiding behind some large crates.

“Come on.” Simms said. “You guys need to get out of here. This whole place is going to come down.”

“No way.” One of the guys said. “That...that thing is out there.”

“Yeah. It’ll get us.” Another guy said.

“Well, it’s about to be in here. Along with the entire building.” Regan said.

“You stay here and you’ll die.” Simms said grabbing one of the men by the arm. The man stood up and allowed himself to be pulled out from behind the crates. Regan grabbed another guy and then all the rest followed. There was a wild scramble through increasing rubble scattered about the warehouse as the group made it’s way out through the large delivery doors.

They just cleared the big doors when, with a loud screeching of metal, the center of the roof of the building collapsed into a giant pile of twisted steel and shattered lumber. A great dust cloud engulfed the guys as they continued to run away from the destroyed warehouse. A writhing tentacle wiggle around in the debris searching for anything of interest, which seemed primarily to be people.

“Go.” Simms said giving a couple of the warehouse workers a shove away from the waterfront. The guys ran up the street and disappeared around a corner.

Regan watched the tentacle knocking debris around in the crushed warehouse. “We aren’t observing much from here.”

"Agreed." Simms said. He waved in the direction the workers had run off in. "Let's get a little further back. Maybe we can see better by not being so close."

"Right." Regan said.

They moved up to the corner and stopped.

"Do you hear that?" Simms asked.

"Yeah." Regan answered. "I just thought it was you breathing hard."

"Funny." Simms said.

"There." Regan pointed down towards the next street corner. There was a soldier with a flamethrower. He was starting to shoot flames at the tentacle. The sound of the flamethrower was like the sound of a loud exhale.

It quickly became apparent that the tentacle was sensitive to the heat of the flame. With each stream of fire the tentacle jerked backwards and the soldier was making progress in pushing the tentacle back towards the waterfront.

Simms and Regan watched the soldier's progress. He seemed to be doing well until he stopped to adjust one of the straps holding the flamethrower on his back. In that moment the tentacle flicked forward and knocked the soldier to the ground. From where they were at it was difficult to tell if the soldier was dead or alive, but he clearly wasn't moving.

"Come on." Simms said as he slapped Regan's arm and started running towards the fallen soldier.

When they reached the soldier the tentacle was waving around over the soldier as if testing to see if the fire had stopped.

"Get it's attention. Distract it. I'm going to grab that soldier and the flamethrower." Simms said.

"I don't really want it's attention, but OK." Regan said. He pulled his gun out and crept closer. He started firing at the tentacle. While the bullets didn't seem to affect it much the tentacle swung in Regan's direction.

Simms dove in and grabbed the soldier by the shoulders and pulled him off to the side of the street. A quick check told Simms the soldier was still alive, but unconscious. He quickly worked the flamethrower off the soldier and started slipping into it. A yell drew his attention. He saw Regan had been knocked aside by the creature's tentacle. He was laying in a small pile of rubble from the collapsed warehouse. The tentacle was rising up above Regan for what appeared to be a crushing slap.

Simms moved out into the street and let loose a stream of fire. The tentacle, in the midst of it's downward arc, jerked backwards. Simms moved in closer and, at that range, scorched the tentacle. With uncanny speed the tentacle shot back down the street, through the debris of the warehouse and disappeared into the water.

Simms dropped the flamethrower and went over to Regan. He was sitting in some rubble. Regan's right hand seemed to be feeling around at his left shoulder.

"Are you OK?" Simms asked.

Regan glanced up at Simms. "A high percentage of me is."

"What percent isn't OK?" Simms said.

Regan waved around his left shoulder. "This percentage."

Simms helped Regan stand up. "Are you OK to keep going?"

Regan nodded. "Yeah. Just don't ask me to wrestle that thing. I'm not sure I could it with one good arm."

"Deal." Simms said. "Come on. Let's circle around this mess to the docks and get a look at this thing from further along the waterfront."

They circled around the remnants of the warehouse and walked out on to the wide dock which this far from the creature was still intact. They got a good view of the giant octopus as it hugged the broken clock tower. Most of the octopus' body was out of the water, but as they watched it was starting to slide back into the ocean. It was impossible to know if it just needed to breathe or the other flamethrowers that were attacking every tentacle that had ventured down the streets were convincing it to abandon the city.

They watched the creature slip down under the surface.

"Out there." Simms pointed out towards a fading ripple on the surface of the water.

"Is that where Mathews' sub is?" Regan asked.

"I would guess so." Simms said.

"Seems pretty damned closed, if you ask me." Regan said.

"Agreed." Simms said.

They stood watching for a little while. Nothing seemed to be happening. Finally there was a small explosion and some bubbles.

"Was that it?" Regan asked.

Simms shook his head. "No. That was definitely too small. Not sure what that was."

They waited, but all was quiet for a little while again.

"Seems like something should have happened by now if everything went according to plan." Regan commented.

"I agree." Simms said. "But there's not much we can do from here."

Another couple of minutes passed and then there was a churning of water. Clearly the creature was thrashing about, but there was nothing on the surface to indicate what the cause of it was.

Finally another much larger explosion sent a geyser of water into the air.

"Now that was it." Regan said.

"The question is: did they kill it?" Simms said.

They walked down as far as they could along the dock until they reached an area that had been destroyed.

"Can't tell from here." Regan said.

"No." Simms agreed. "Let's see if we can get ourselves over to the naval base and meet Mathews and the sub."

9

Simms and Regan stood back as Lesley hugged Captain Mathews as he and Carter walked off the plank that led down to the submarine.

"I'm so glad you are OK." Lesley said. "John radioed me that you nearly died down there getting the octopus to let the ship go."

Mathews shrugged. "All part of the job."

"Yes, well normally the captain stays inside the ship." Carter commented with a smile.

Mathews turned to Simms and Regan. "Well, gentlemen, I suspect your work here is done."

"Maybe." Simms said. "We have to determine the cause of the trouble near Hawaii, but if that turns out to be a false alarm then it would seem like we are finished here."

"Well, we are going out for a celebratory dinner and we would like you two to join us." Carter said giving Simms and Regan a friendly slap on the back.

"Perhaps we can join you later." Simms said. "We need to check on those interviews from Pearl and our office first."

"Very well. Hopefully we'll see you later then." Mathews said and Lesley and Carter headed up the dock with him.

"You really think this thing is over?" Regan asked skeptically.

Simms shook his head. "No, but they seemed so happy at the thought that it was I didn't want to ruin their celebration."

They headed back to the Naval Headquarters and headed into the large office area. As soon as they walked in a sailor came up to them.

"Sir, I can't find Doctor Carter, but this came in from Pearl for him." The sailor handed Simms a slip of paper.

Simms read it. "Damn." He handed the paper over to Regan.

Regan read it. "Crap. It sounds like those Chinese sailors are pretty damned sure it was some kind of monster that attacked them."

"Yeah." Simms said. "I need to let the Director know we are headed back to Hawaii."

"Uh, OK, while you are doing that I think I will check in and see how Beka is doing." Regan said hesitantly.

Simms looked at Regan dubiously. "I thought that whole business was resolved."

Regan shook his head. "She doesn't know anyone here. She has nowhere to go."

Simms stared at Regan for a minute. He glanced at his watch. "First, you need to have a doctor look at that shoulder. Then a *brief* stop in Sausilito and then meet me back here by six. I've got to talk to the Director and then probably Admiral Burns to arrange whatever we need back in Pearl."

"Right." Regan said and headed out of the building.

An hour later Simms and Admiral Burns walked into the restaurant.

"Over there." Burns pointed. They wove their way through the tables.

"Admiral Burns." Mathews stood up and saluted. "Good of you to join our little celebration."

Burns shook his head slightly. "I'm afraid we're not quite ready to celebrate."

"Oh, not again." Carter said. This was their second attempt to enjoy an evening meal and celebrate an achievement. The first time was just after they had identified what the creature was and Carter and Lesley were expecting to head off to a conference in Cairo. Instead they had been detained to battle a giant octopus.

"I'm afraid so." Burns said. "It's been confirmed that something big attacked that Chinese freighter near Hawaii."

"Really, Admiral, why do you need us?" Lesley asked.

"Well, to be perfectly honest, I wasn't coming here to ask you two to help us deal with this new creature. You've already gone above and beyond what could be expected. Our colleagues in the OSO," Burns waved a hand towards Simms, "are going to head back to Hawaii with us. I am here to inform Captain Mathews that his submarine ships out by 0100 hours. But your help in dealing with this new threat would, of course, be greatly appreciated by the Navy."

Mathews looked down at Lesley. She was staring up at him.

"Captain, you should probably get to your ship." Burns said.

Mathews tore his gaze away from Lesley. "Yes sir."

Lesley stood up. "If Pete's ship is going back to Pearl, well, I'll go too. I'll help in any way I can."

Mathews smiled at Lesley.

"Aw, hell, I might as well go too." Carter said standing up.

"Good. I was hoping you two would come along." Burns said.

Carter looked at Simms. "I think I understand now why we have the OSO. These monsters just keep showing up."

"Does seem that way." Simms agreed.

A short time later the whole group returned to the Naval headquarters. They filed into the large office area. Simms was the last one into the room and he stopped when he walked in. Regan was already there and waiting. Simms walked slowly over to Regan.

"Hmm." Simms said. He glanced at Regan's left arm as it sat in a sling. Then, with a sigh, his eyes turned to Beka.

"Hey, Boss. Ready for duty." Beka said with a salute and a smile.

Simms looked at Regan. "No."

Regan nodded. "I tried that word. Several times. Didn't seem to get me anywhere."

Simms looked at Beka. "No."

Beka shrugged. "I was already in Hawaii. You guys dragged me to San Francisco."

"First," Simms said, "*we* didn't drag you here and second, I don't think anyone can drag you anywhere."

"Well, I can't argue with the second part." Beka said.

"We're not a travel agency. If you want to go back to Hawaii you need to make your own arrangements." Simms said.

"Don't be silly. You guys need me." Beka said.

"Need you? What are you talking about?" Simms asked.

Beka pointed at Regan's arm. "The moment you two are out of my sight look what happens."

"Elliot." Regan said. When Simms looked at him, Regan shook his head. "Save yourself a lot of grief. Let it go."

Simms sighed. "I'm beginning to look forward to the monsters."

10

Shortly after the plane landed at the Pearl Harbor Naval base they found themselves back where it had all started, in the lab where Carter and Lesley first identified the creature.

"So what was it the sailor was telling us has happened?" Carter asked.

"He says a Navy ship was attacked just south of here early this morning." Simms said.

"Did I hear right? Someone got pictures of it?" Carter held the door for everyone as they entered the building.

Simms stopped in the lobby of the Research building and turned to face Carter. "Yeah. Apparently the ship, a destroyer, drove the creature off, but someone on deck got pictures of the attack. They rushed the pictures through development and they are supposed to be waiting for us here."

The sailor at the front desk glanced up at them, but said nothing. They walked back to the lab and on one of the long tables in the lab were some pictures sitting in a pile. Lesley and Carter leaned over the pile while Simms and Regan flanked the other two. Beka tried to peek past Regan's should, but gave up after a couple of attempts.

There were 9 pictures and Carter examined each one before sliding it slowly aside and looking at the next.

"Looks like the ship was being rocked about some." Carter commented.

"He was having a hard time getting a clear shot of it." Simms said in agreement.

"It never breaks the surface." Carter said as he scanned the last photo. "From what I can tell there were definitely tentacles reaching up around the ship."

"Wait." Lesley said. "Go back a couple of pictures."

Carter slid back through the photos.

"There." Lesley stopped Carter on a particular picture and pointed up at a corner of the picture.

Carter looked a little closer. "You're right. That's...that's distinctive."

"Maybe you could share the distinctiveness of it with us?" Regan asked.

"Oh, here. Look at the shape of this." Carter said running his finger along something in the corner of the picture.

"I'm trying to get excited about that, but somehow..." Regan said.

"That's the end of a tentacle and it's clearly not the tentacle of an octopus." Lesley said.

"So what is it?" Simms asked.

"A giant squid." Carter said confidently.

"Aren't those natural creatures?" Regan asked.

Carter nodded slightly. "Yes, but as a rule they don't generally get big enough to threaten a Navy destroyer."

"So this is probably another creature from the Mindanao Deep?" Simms asked.

Lesley slowly nodded her head. "I'm afraid we will have to assume so."

"I agree." Carter said.

"How long before Captain Mathews and his sub arrive?" Simms asked.

"Pete said he would be here sometime tomorrow." Lesley answered.

"Well, we have until tomorrow then to come up a plan for killing this creature." Simms said.

"You mean something better than running up to it with a flamethrower?" Beka asked gently patting Regan's shoulder.

"Yeah." Simms said. "Something better than that."

The following morning Simms walked into the lab in the Research building to find Carter and Lesley hard at work.

"Am I to assume you have come up with something?" Simms asked them.

Carter nodded. "After our encounter in San Francisco I am thinking maybe using explosives at close range might not be the best approach."

"That did seem like a bit of a close call." Simms agreed.

"Too close." Lesley added. She looked anxious and tired.

Simms stared at Lesley for moment. "You're worried about Captain...Pete going after this creature in the sub."

Lesley ran a hand through her hair. "It shows I guess." She gave Simms a weak smile.

Simms returned her smile. "Robbie and I are going to be on that sub with him and we have every intention of getting back here all in one piece."

"I will be there too." Carter said, resting a hand on Lesley's shoulder.

Lesley smiled again. "Thank you."

Regan and Beka walked in. Simms turned and watched them.

"Morning Boss." Beka said.

"Sleep well?" Simms asked Regan.

"Uh, yeah. Fine." Regan said. Regan shuffled a little uncomfortably. He and Simms were sharing a room on the base, but he had not spent the night in that room.

Somewhere during the night Simms had come to terms with the situation. He recognized that they weren't machines, the agents of the OSO, and Regan wasn't the first one to demonstrate that. Agent Wyatt was known to be living with a girl he had met on his so called vacation in Indonesia.

Simms gave Regan a quick smile and turned back to Carter. "So what is this new plan for this creature."

"We're thinking a high enough dose of a neurological toxin will do the trick." Carter said.

"It will stop the creature's breathing." Lesley added.

"So it essentially suffocates." Simms said.

"Exactly." Carter said.

"How long to get it ready?" Simms asked.

"We already have all the poison extracted from Pterois Volitans we could get a hold of on it's way here." Carter said. "It should do the trick nicely. Very toxic."

"Terry who?" Beka asked.

"The Lionfish." Lesley said.

"Will it be enough?" Simms asked.

"Should be. As I said, it is very toxic. We should have enough to easily take down something as big as this creature appears to be." Carter said.

"So, back to my question, how long before you are ready?" Simms asked.

"Well, we should have the toxin here by this afternoon and we have some guys working on retro fitting a torpedo to act as a giant syringe. I think by day's end we should be ready." Carter said.

"Does Captain Mathews know of the plan?" Simms said.

"Yes. I talked to him a little earlier." Lesley said.

Simms nodded. "Good. Now we just have to hope our large friend remains in these waters long enough for us to find him."

11

"I thought we were headed down to the docks to meet the sub?" Regan asked as the car left the Naval base and headed north along the shore.

"We are, but just before we walked out I got a message indicating there were several whale carcasses washed ashore north of here. If we can confirm that they were killed by our giant squid then we can be sure he is still in the area." Carter explained.

"Ugh. Whale carcasses. Why do we seemed to always have to go look at those things?" Regan said.

Simms, sitting next to Regan in the backseat, nodded. "Hard to get that smell out of your nose after you've been up close to them."

Carter laughed. "Yeah. It is a little rough."

It took them only about twenty minutes to find the right beach. They parked and walked down to the water. There was a whale and a half washed up on the beach. Simms and Regan kept their distance under the pretext of staying out of Cater and Lesley's way. It didn't take long for Lesley and Carter to return.

"Well?" Simms asked.

Carter nodded. "Definitely Architeuthidae."

"Is that a yes or no?" Regan asked.

"That's a yes." Lesley said with a smile. "It's a giant squid that killed these whales."

"So, it's still around here." Simms said.

"Looks that way." Carter said. "We ought to be able to lure it to us with some bait. It will make our job a lot easier."

Regan nodded. "Sure. It's always easier to find a monster when you can entice it to chase you. The hard part is not getting eaten by it."

In a short time they were parked near the docks back on the Naval base. The submarine had already docked and people were quickly shuttling to and from the sub preparing it for a quick turnaround. The four of them, Carter, Lesley, Simms and Regan wound their way along the walkways towards the sub. Lesley was in front and Carter reached a hand out stopping Simms and Regan.

"Let's give them a moment." Carter said nodding to Lesley hurrying down to meet Mathews.

Simms was a little unsure what was going on. He watched Lesley and Mathews kiss and Mathews talking to Lesley. The conversation seemed serious.

"Is there a problem?" Simms asked Carter.

"That depends on someone's answer." Carter said with a smile.

Mathews and Lesley embraced. They turned and walked up the dock to the others.

Simms still looked confused, but Regan seemed to catch on.

"So, I take it congratulations are in order?" Carter asked.

Lesley smiled at Mathews. "Yes, they are."

"Well, it's about time." Carter said.

"Uh...?" Simms hesitated.

"They're getting married." Regan said quietly into Simms' ear.

"Oh. Uh, congratulations." Simms said.

"Thank you." Lesley said. "Where's Beka?"

Regan shrugged. "She had some personal stuff here to deal with."

"So tell me about this new torpedo you have for me." Mathews said to Carter.

Carter pointed at some sailors standing further up the dock around a large cart covered with a tarp. "It's over here."

They all walked over to take another look at the weapon.

"How long before we're ready to ship back out?" Mathews asked.

"A couple of hours and we should be ready to go." Carter answered.

It took three hours, but the sub slipped out of it's moorings and headed out of the harbor. They moved through a standard search pattern in a wide circling of Hawaii and for six hours found nothing.

"Why do none of these pipes running overhead contain coffee?" Regan asked as they all crammed in around the sonar as best they could.

Mathews laughed. "That's an excellent idea. I'll bring that up with the Admiralty when we get back."

"Something sir." The sonar operator said.

Mathews leaned in. "What does it look like?"

"Not sure, sir." The sonar operator answered. "It looks big."

"Well, follow it. Try to make out what we're looking at." Mathews said.

"Yes sir." The sonar operator said.

Carter stared at the screen. "That doesn't look right."

"Why do you say that?" Simms asked.

"It's moving too slow. It's turning slow too." Carter replied. "Doesn't have the characteristics I would expect from our target."

"I think it's a school of fish, sir." The sonar operator said.

"I would agree." Carter said.

"I don't think I have ever seen one that large before." The sailor running the sonar said. "It's like all the fish are running in the same direction."

Carter glanced at Mathews.

"Like something's chasing them." Mathews said.

Carter nodded. "But...that would suggest that we are between—-"

The whole sub suddenly lurched to one side and then came to an abrupt stop. Everyone was thrown forward and crashed into various consoles and equipment. They struggled back to their feet and looked around at each other.

"What the hell...?" Regan said.

"Damn." Mathews said. "I am getting painfully familiar with this situation." He wiped away a little blood from a small cut on his forehead.

"I would guess the creature we are searching for has found us." Carter said.

"I would agree." Mathews said. "The problem is, our special torpedo fires from the bow and I believe our friend has a hold of us from the stern."

"We need to convince him to let go so we can turn around." Simms said.

"Right." Mathews said. He went over and grabbed the communications mic. "Engine room."

"Yes sir." Came the answer.

"I want you to flush some oil out." Mathews said.

"Aye aye sir."

It took several minutes before they heard an odd hissing sound and another minute before they felt a jerk and the submarine seemed roll slightly to one side.

"Flank speed. Bring us about as quick as you can." Mathews shouted.

"Aye sir."

Mathews grabbed the mic again. "Torpedo room. Get our special package ready."

"Aye aye sir."

"Sonar, let me know when you have fix on our friend." Mathews said.

"Yes sir."

They could feel the sub swinging around.

"Sir, I have the—-" The sonar operator started to say.

The ship lurched again and once again everyone was sent crashing about.

"That's getting kind of tiring." Regan said picking himself back up.

"I am guessing we are in it's grasp again." Carter said glancing around the compartment as if he could see the tentacles holding the submarine.

Mathews sighed. "Yeah. Sonar, where's our target?"

"Dead ahead, sir." Was the answer.

"Well, thank goodness for small miracles." Mathews said. He grabbed the communication mic again. "Torpedo room. Are we ready with that torpedo?"

"Aye sir. Tube one is ready."

"Flood tube one." Mathews ordered.

"Tube one flooded, sir." Came the voice over the speaker.

"Fire tube one." Mathews said.

Everyone heard the swoosh sound of the tube being fired.

"Tube one fired."

Everyone stood silent for a moment.

"Uh, without an explosion, how we know if we hit it?" Regan asked.

"At this range, I don't know if we could miss it." Mathews said.

"So how we know if it worked?" Simms asked.

"Oh, I am sure that the poison will work." Carter said. "It won't take long for the neurological toxin to paralyze the creature."

"We should be able to see it sink to the bottom on the sonar." Mathews said, leaning back over to the sonar screen.

A shudder ran through the submarine.

"What was that?" Regan asked.

"I believe our toxin is having it's effect upon our friend out there." Carter said. "It won't be long now and our troubles will be over."

Suddenly the angle of the submarine tilted down. Everyone grabbed hold of something to prevent themselves from sliding towards the front of the compartment.

"Sir, we're dropping." One of the sailors called out.

"Damn it." Mathews said. "It's not dead?"

"I think it is dead." Simms said. "I just think it didn't let go of us."

Everyone exchanged quick glances.

"What's our depth?" Mathews called out.

"3-5-0 and dropping fast sir." Came the answer.

"How deep is it here?" Simms asked.

Mathews hesitated and thought for a moment. "About 3200 feet."

"What's the crush depth of this ship?" Simms asked.

Mathews hesitated again. "2500."

"I am not really liking the difference between those two numbers." Regan said.

"Yeah. Neither am I." Mathews said.

"How close can you set a timer on a torpedo?" Simms asked.

Mathews looked at Simms for a moment. He nodded. "Pretty damn close."

"Depth 1-4-0-0. Still dropping fast." Came a voice.

Mathews turned and grabbed the communication mic. "Torpedo room. How short a timer can you set? Is it ten seconds?"

"15 sir." Came the answer.

"That's a good ways out there." Carter said.

"Yeah. Probably too far past our friend." Mathews said. "not much choice, though. If we're lucky we'll hit the thing and that might keep it close enough to knock it loose."

"There...is another issue." Simms said.

"Oh, what's that?" Mathews asked.

"What if the torpedo can't clear the tube?" Simms asked.

"Clear the tube?" Mathews looked at Simms.

"He means, what if the creature's tentacle is blocking the tube?" Carter clarified.

"Oh, well, then I guess we're still headed for the bottom." Mathews said.

"Delightful." Regan said.

"Limited choices." Simms said.

"Right." Mathews nodded. He lifted the mic again. "Torpedo room. Prep tube one and set the timer for 15 seconds."

"Aye aye sir."

"Depth 2-1-0-0. Still dropping." A voice called out.

"Tube one ready sir." Came a voice out of the speaker.

Mathews glanced at everyone and then turned back to the communications panel. "Fire tube one."

There was the familiar swoosh sound.

"Guess we cleared the tube." Carter said.

"Yes, but how far?" Simms asked.

"Torpedo running." The sonar operator said.

"That's good. Now if we just don't go too—-" Carter started saying.

"Torpedo stopped." The sonar operator cut in.

"Did we hit it?" Regan asked.

Mathews was looking at his watch. "Won't know until about—-"

There was boom and the submarine shook. Everyone was tossed from the left to the right.

"Depth 2-4-0-0 and slowing."

"You think we're free?" Carter wondered.

"Blow ballasts. Surface." Mathews called out.

"Blowing ballasts." Came a reply.

Everyone stood still for a minute.

"Depth 2-2-5-0 and rising." Came another voice.

There was a collective sigh.

"You think it's dead?" Simms asked Carter.

"I think we have to assume it is." Carter answered.

"Good enough for me. Let's go home." Mathews said. "I have a wedding to figure out."

12

The plane banked around and headed east. Simms sat back and closed his eyes for a moment. He was very tired. The flight from Hawaii was long and he hadn't been able to get much sleep. Now the flight from San Francisco to Chicago and then on to Washington DC from there was going to be even longer.

There was an uneasy feeling in the pit of his stomach. Perhaps it was the uncertainty about whether there were any more of those creatures from the Mindanao Deep lurking out in the Pacific. A part of him knew it was more than just that. Recently the OSO had been busier than usual. As if things in this world were spinning faster and faster out of control. He didn't know, but he couldn't shake that feeling. It was something he felt he needed to talk to Marcus about when he got back to DC.

"I am sure glad to be rid of that sling." Regan said, flexing his arm in the seat next to Simms.

"I'm sure." Simms replied.

"You think there's any more of those things out there?" Regan asked.

"I don't know." Simms said wearily, glancing over at Regan. "We've got a long flight. We should probably get some rest."

"True enough." Regan said leaning back in his seat.

"Sure thing, Boss." Beka said leaning forward a little to look at Simms from the seat next to Regan.

Simms leaned back again and closed his eyes with a sigh. That woman, Simms thought, does not know the meaning of the word "No".

K McConnell

For more information about other stories, including more free stories to download, please visit www.kmcconnellbooks.com

Also, if you enjoyed this story, please feel free to send any thoughts or comments to kmcconnell@kmcconnellbooks.com

Other books by K McConnell

The Hamlet Mysteries series...

To Not Be In Hamlet

Sam MacNeil, part time mystery writer, has returned to his hometown to house sit for his parents as they start a lengthy vacation. What Sam has forgotten while away is the quirky weirdness of the little town of Hamlet. With expectations that he would quietly do his time in Hamlet the discovery of a dead body, clearly murdered, changes everything. Now Sam finds, much to his chagrin, the residents of Hamlet are expecting him to solve the murder. Not only does Sam not want to be involved in it, but the authroities have made it clear his help is not wanted. Was it the angry businessman from Detroit? Was it the shifty handyman the victim worked with? Sam doesn't know, but when killers from Detroit show up the situation is taking a serious and deadly turn. And then there's Becky. An old friend who clearly has more than friendship on her mind. Murder, killers and romance...this is not how this brief stay in Hamlet was supposed to go.

The Art of Hamlet

An old family friend asks Sam to look into a break in at her house. She is an art collector and critic, but nothing has been stolen and the only thing disturbed are some small statues. While it is a puzzling incident Sam doesn't think it is a serious issue, but when a neighbor is murdered and found bobbing in a nearby lake the story is once again taking a dark turn. As usual Sam is not inclined to get involved in a murder investigation, but somehow he seems to be sliding in that direction anyway. In addition, the County Detective seems to have recognized that Sam might be of some use—-regardless of the consequences for Sam. And what of Sam's old classmate, who is now a seemingly crazy hermit, ranting on about terrorists in Hamlet? Is that actually possible? To complicate things even further something is happening between Sam and Becky. Love and Death seem to be chasing Sam through the wacky streets of Hamlet.

Ophelia's Hunt

Sam's women troubles have seemingly tripled. There is Becky and the relationship that Sam has found himself in with her. However, suddenly, there is Callie. Sam's wealthy and wild ex-fiance who has appeared in Hamlet. Is she here to get Sam back? Everyone thinks so—-including Becky. Then there's the beautiful woman named Misty. She seems to have a particular interest in Sam as well. And, of course, there's murder in Hamlet once again. Questions abound. Is the lovely Misty a suspect or a new love interest? Who are the men stalking Callie? How is Sam going explain all of this to an increasingly angry Becky? Why is the County Detective actually soliciting Sam's help? Should Sam be flattered or very careful? With love and murder swirling around Sam how is he going to survive this?

The Ghosts of Hamlet

Sam MacNeil, part time writer, is house sitting for his parents in his hometown of Hamlet. The people of Hamlet are far more quirky than Sam remembers from his childhood and he is keen on leaving them behind and getting his life back, but it's those dead bodies that are the real problem. They just keep showing up. Murder in the small town of Hamlet has taken a noticeable uptick since Sam has returned and the residents have taken notice. Sam claims it has nothing to do with him and yet...Now, even worse, the residents are seeing ghosts and they blame Sam for that as well.

Sam may get his chance to escape Hamlet now that his parents are heading home, but can he really walk away without solving the mystery of the ghosts? Will he get away before the "gangsters" from Detroit catch up with him and turn him into a ghost? And what about Becky? He really wasn't planning on a romantic entanglement to muddle things up.

So what do ghosts, gangsters, girlfriends, musk ox and talking cans of beans all have in common? Sam MacNeil and the quirky town of Hamlet, of course.

The Play of Hamlet

It is finally here. The Founder's Day festival in Hamlet. A gala event highlighted by a play depicting the bizarre founding of Hamlet. Sam is not only the star of the play, but also a target for Scanlon and his killers from Detroit. They are determined to finish him off once and for all. But Sam knows they are coming and, with the help of the quirky residents of Hamlet, he has his own plans in the works. What Sam doesn't know is that Scanlon isn't the only killer from Sam's past that is out to get him. Could the biggest day of the year in Hamlet be Sam's last?

The King of Hamlet

The sixth story in the Hamlet Mystery series starts out where most of the stories end up...with a dead body. The trouble is Sam is found standing over the dead body and refusing to explain what has happened. He seems willing to take the fall for the guy's murder, but he is clearly hiding something. His friends are sure he didn't commit murder, but who is he protecting and why? What Sam is not telling anyone is that he is playing a more dangerous game than any of them can imagine. As bodies begin piling up around Sam he is increasingly wondering if he has a guardian angel or has become an unwilling accomplice to the Angel of Death. Once again women and murder are causing headaches for Sam.

The Graves of Hamlet

As if the town of Hamlet didn't have enough trouble with dead bodies now, it appears, someone is digging them up in the cemetary. The quirky residents of Hamlet are sure this has something to do with Sam. As usual Sam doesn't really want anything to do with whatever is going on, but when someone tries to make the cemetary Sam's premanent home one dark night it would seem that Sam will need to sort this out—-if only to save himself. To add to the confusion, with Becky out of town, Sam must also figure out who the half naked woman is that keeps showing up on his deck sun bathing. Oh, and who are these other guys that just showed up in Hamlet? The grandson of the recently deceased retired cop who is lying about his real identity and the suspicious looking guy casually asking questions around town about the same dead cop...?

Polonius' Plight

Here's a surprise...there's been a murder in Hamlet—-again. This time, however, Sam is very much intentionally involved. It's the suspects. The guy was found with a gaping shotgun blast to the chest. Like the one in the trunk of Renee's car. Of course the last person to be seen with the murder victim was Jen—-and she seems to have disappeared. And why is Reese, the County Detective looking for Becky and her grandfather's .38? Sam is sure none of his friends are murderers, but to keep any and all of them out of jail he needs to find out who the killer is and fast. To make matters worse, while Sam is trying to solve a murder and hide his friends the Town Council of Hamlet has had enough of Sam and the murders that seem to follow him around. They passed yet another of their many bizarre ordinances. Sam has been ordered to leave Hamlet.

The Office of Scientific Operations

With the conclusion of the traumatic events in 1933 surrounding the shocking affair involving the city of New York and a beast commonly referred to as "King Kong", the president of the United States, Franklin Roosevelt, established the Office of Scientific Operations (OSO). The purpose of the OSO was to monitor and evaluate the level of risk and assist in any manner the mitigation of danger of any and all scientific operations and anomalies. With the rapid pace of scientific discovery this office was given the highest priority and clearance to investigate any potential threats or consequences to the interests of the United States of America.

What follows are the real stories behind the cinematic cover-ups presented to the general public...

Release #1 from the declassified files of the Office of Scientific Operations...

From 1953...

File #153 (commonly referred to by the public as "The Beast from 20,000 Fathoms")

OSO agents Elliot Simms and Robbie Regan, while observing an atomic test in the Arctic, are unwittingly caught up in the release of prehistoric beasts from millions of years of suspended animation in the ice. Now they must help in stopping this new terror as it moves steadily down the east coast destroying anything in it's path.

From 1954...

File #157 (commonly referred to by the public as "Them")

OSO agents Simms and Regan investigate the odd circumstances surrounding a missing FBI agent only to stumble upon a horror in the New Mexico desert and if they cannot find a way to stop it there is a very good chance this could be the end of humanity.

Release #2
from the declassified files of the
Office of Scientific Operations...

From 1954...

File #159 (commonly referred to by the public as "Terror in the Jungle")

OSO agent Jonathon Wyatt is pulled off vacation to an island in Indonesia to investigate sightings of pteranodons. The island is not far from the island known infamously as Z Land. It was once the headquarters of Dr. Zeitner whose experiments in genetically manipulating prehistoric monsters terrorized the world in the 1930s before the OSO put a stop to it. Wyatt's job is to determine if these are indeed Dr. Zeitner's creatures, but what he finds is much more deadly. This is no way to spend a vacation—-trying not to get eaten.

Release #3
from the declassified files of the Office of Scientific Operations...

From 1954...

File #161 (commonly referred to by the public as "Revenge of the Creature")

After the capture of an unknown species of half man half fish is brought back to a Florida marine institute, OSO agents Wayne and Wyatt must determine the risk to the American people it poses. When the creature escapes and begins terrorizing the citizens of Florida the risk becomes all too real. Now they must hunt it down and stop it's killing spree, if they can.

From 1955...

File #165 (commonly referred to by the public as "It Came From Beneath the Sea")

OSO agents Simms and Regan are sent out to Pearl Harbor to investigate damage to one of the Navy's most advanced atomic submarines by some kind of giant creature. While the Navy has a hard time believing it, the OSO knows such creatures are real. It soon becomes apparent by the large number of ships being lost that something dangerous is hunting throughout the Pacific. Now, with the creature openly attacking the west coast of the United States Simms and Regan join the fight to stop this thing before the entire Pacific is destroyed by it.

Release #4

from the declassified files of the

Office of Scientific Operations...

From 1954...

File #163 (commonly referred to by the public as "The DC Creeper")

On a break from hunting monsters for the Office of Scientific Operations, OSO Agent Wyatt is trying to adjust to a more crowded domestic life. As brutally murdered bodies begin showing up in the nation's capitol, though, this doesn't seem like it is going to be much of a break. The newspapers have dubbed the hulking killer "The Creeper" and it looks like Wyatt is going to have to hunt him down and stop him before Wyatt becomes the next victim.

Release #5
from the declassified files of the
Office of Scientific Operations...

From 1956...

File #166 (commonly referred to by the public as "Tarantula")

Agents Simms and Regan from the Office of Scientific Operations, the OSO, returning from the Pacific Coast having just finished dealing with yet another monster threatening the United States are redirected to a small town in Arizona to verify that a large tarantula that has been terrorizing the local inhabitants has been destroyed by the Air Force. With Beka, a woman who insists on tagging along with the intrepid agents—-a clear violation of official regulations—-in tow, they quickly discover that the threat of the giant spiders in the Arizona desert are not over just yet.

From 1956...

File #171 (commonly referred to by the public as "Invasion of the Body Snatchers")

The Office of Scientific Operations, the OSO, has sent agents Wayne and Wyatt out to the small California city of Santa Mira to locate a missing Air Force major, sent to investigate the impact of some meteors, and to understand the meaning of his last cryptic message to Washington. What they find is that, while the city of Santa Mira may look like a quaint place to visit it soon becomes apparent that a missing Air Force major is the least of Wayne and Wyatt's problems. There is something very strange and deadly going on in Santa Mira. Something that seems...alien?

The New Sheriff

Travis Ames, somehow, has developed super powers. Exactly what these powers entail he's not sure. He's still learning how to control his powers, but he's already decided that he should use this new found power to fight crime. And...if he made a little profit along the way, well, that wouldn't be so bad either. But reality has a way of altering the best laid plans. He has quickly figured out he has no idea how to go about crime fighting. And, to make matters worse, he has learned the hard way, his new powers won't protect him from getting hurt or, quite possibly, killed. Can he survive long enough to learn how to use his powers? Can he get an aging detective to teach him how to fight crime? Can he prevent Aubrey, the new girl, and everyone else at work from figuring out what he can do? How long can he keep this up before he makes that one small mistake and ends up dead?

Also by K McConnell

Office of Scientific Operations

Office of Scientific Operations - Release #1

The Hamlet Mysteries

The Hamlet Mysteries 1

The Hamlet Mysteries 3

Standalone

A Conspiracy in Blood

Symbiotic Puppets

The Plague

The Club of the Bombastic Few

The Master Switch

Hamlet On A Budget

The New Sheriff

Office of Scientific Operations - Declassified Files (Release #2)

Office of Scientific Operations Release #3

Office of Scientific Operations - Declassified Files (Release #4)

Office of Scientific Operations - Declassified Files (Release #5)

The Hamlet Mysteries 2

Office of Scientific Operations - Release #6

The Hamlet Mysteries 1 - 9

The Trench of the Dead

The Heart of a Monster

Watch for more at www.kmcconnellbooks.com.

www.ingramcontent.com/pod-product-compliance
Lightning Source LLC
LaVergne TN
LVHW091045150826
845673LV00002B/469